The Willows
and Beyond

THE TALES OF THE WILLOWS

By Kenneth Grahame
The Wind in the Willows

By William Horwood
The Willows in Winter
Toad Triumphant
The Willows and Beyond

ALSO BY WILLIAM HORWOOD

The Duncton Wood Series
The Stonor Eagles
Callanish
Skallagrigg
The Wolves of time

WILLIAM HORWOOD

The Willows and Beyond

Illustrated by Patrick Benson

Thomas Dunne Books/St. Martin's Griffin
New York

THOMAS DUNNE BOOKS.
An imprint of St. Martin's Press.

Library of Congress Cataloging-in-Publication Data

Horwood, William.
  The willows and beyond / William Horwood ; illustrated by Patrick Benson.
    p.   cm.
  "Thomas Dunne books."
  Third book in a series continuing the story of: The wind in the willows by
Kenneth Grahame.
  Sequel to: Toad triumphant.
  Summary: Continues the adventures of Toad, Mole, Rat and Badger as they
reminisce about their past escapades and prepare to turn over the River Bank to
the next generation.
  ISBN 0-312-19365-3 (hc)
  ISBN 0-312-24497-5 (pbk)
  [1. Animals—Fiction. 2. Friendship—Fiction. 3. England—Fiction.]   I. Benson,
Patrick, ill.   II. Grahame, Kenneth, 1859–1932.   Wind in the willows.   III. Title.
PZ7.H7928Wg   1998
[Fic]—dc21   98-26150
                                                                      CIP
                                                                       AC

First published in Great Britain by HarperCollins*Publishers*

First St. Martin's Griffin Edition: October 1999

10 9 8 7 6 5 4 3 2 1

Contents

· I ·
The River's Warning

It was late September, and after a week of storms and rain, which had caused the River to rise, and the once-glorious vegetation along the River Bank to grow old and bedraggled, the sun started to show itself again.

Now, with a new dawn, the day promised a time of calmer, drier weather and the final touch of an Indian summer. A thin veil of mist hung over the River, and all seemed subdued, and at peace.

The Mole, who had not been able to leave Mole End for some days, had left Nephew to busy himself with a few necessary repairs to the windows and doors before winter set in, and had gone off for the day to see his good friend the Water Rat.

He had reached the Iron Bridge and was leaning on its parapet to gaze down at the River, and watch its endless flow, when he noticed some-body sitting a little way along the bank, hardly more than a misty silhouette.

"Is that you, Otter?" he called. "Hello, Mole," said the Otter, rising to join him. Then, seeing the fat wicker luncheon-basket he carried, he added, "You're not off to see Ratty, are you?"

"You can join us if you like," said the hospitable Mole. "Seeing that these are likely to be the last few decent days of summer, I thought —"

"I'd leave Ratty well alone today, if I were you, Mole," said the Otter seriously. "He's communing with the River, and has been since yesterday."

"Aah!" said the Mole, putting down his basket. "Then I'll have to think of something else to do, for at such a time Ratty's best left by himself."

The Otter continued to stare down at the River, and seemed unusually quiet and distracted for one normally so cheerful.

"Is something amiss along the River?" enquired the Mole anxiously.

"I think there may be," said the Otter, "though what it is I cannot say. I have known Ratty commune with

8

the River many times before, we all have, but not for quite so long, and not so . . . so *seriously*.

"I took him some food and a warming drink last evening – I left it nearby where he might see it when he was ready, for I did not wish to disturb him – but I swear it was untouched this morning."

"You mean he has been out all night?" cried the Mole.

"I think he must have been."

"And he seems troubled?"

"Very," said the Otter sombrely.

"Well, we certainly shouldn't disturb him," said the thoughtful Mole, "but we can be at hand when he has finished, for he'll be very tired, and in need of good food and company."

So it was agreed, and the two spent the day at Otter's house, sending Otter's son Portly down-river from time to time to see how Ratty was getting on.

"He's still there, just sitting and staring, and raising his arms occasionally, as he does when he's communing," reported Portly at eleven o'clock, at midday, at two o'clock and again just after three.

"We'll leave it till the end of the afternoon," said the Otter, "and then I'll go along again myself. Meanwhile, Mole, I hope you don't mind if I help myself to some more of that cranberry pie you've made; there'll still be plenty left for Ratty."

"Please have as much as you wish," insisted the Mole, "and for goodness' sake put some of this clotted cream on top, for it just does not taste the same without it."

A little later, Mole went out and gazed down-river

towards the distant form of the Rat in the fading sunlight. "O my," he sighed, and went back to sit by the Otter and wait while the minutes and hours passed by.

Both of them knew that if there were one animal along the River Bank who understood the River's moods better than any other, and who heard its call more clearly than them all, it was the Water Rat. Come spring, summer, autumn or winter, a day rarely went by when the Rat was not either in the water or on it, swimming or sculling, thinking and dreaming. If he did have to be away from the River Bank, for social or business reasons, he was restless and uneasy till he was back in touch with the River again.

For the most part the Rat called the River "she", and none thereabouts doubted where his heart and spirit lay, or what was the source of his deepest joy and happiness, and, for that matter, his sporadic moods and silences. The River-Bankers never questioned the Rat for a single moment on those occasions, happily rare and usually at times of spring and autumn spate, when he warned others off the River, and told them to leave her alone for a time.

His chief confidant and helper in such difficult times was the Otter, who lived as close to the River as the Rat, and was as adept as he in managing her more violent moods of storm and flood. When it came to matters of River history and lore, however, the Otter deferred to the Rat's greater knowledge and wisdom.

It was one of the quiet pleasures of the River Bank to see the Rat and the Otter conferring about the changing mood of the River, sitting upon the bank, their feet dangling in the water, their voices low. Only Portly was allowed to disturb them, for such was the power of the River over them that they sometimes needed reminding that their tea was ready, or they were due at Mole End in half an hour for supper.

It was no wonder then, that the Otter was so concerned about this latest episode. But as the September day wore on into a balmy evening and still Portly reported that there was no change, they began to think that something very serious indeed was afoot.

The Mole was just beginning to consider that he might go home for the night and return in the morning when Portly came running along the bank.

"He's moved! He's up and he's stretched, and he's gone back into his house and shut the door!"

"I think this is a matter for you now, Mole old fellow," said the Otter. "You're a better judge than I as to whether or not Ratty's at home to visitors."

The Mole smiled and said, "Now, how much of that cranberry pie have you left?"

They quickly gathered together what remained of the feast the Mole had prepared, added a few things from the Otter's more workaday larder and set off to see if their friend might be lured back into society.

"Ratty!" called the Mole, having tapped at his door. "Are you there, Ratty?"

"You know perfectly well I am," said an irritable voice from inside Ratty's house.

"Well then, are you at home to visitors? Because I've brought you some —"

The door opened a little and two bright eyes peered out.

"Some what?"

"O, nothing very much, just a little bit of supper, because I had heard —"

"What had you heard?" said the Rat, letting the door open a shade more.

"— and I know that at such times —"

"What do you know about such times?" said the Rat in a more friendly way, and opening his door wider still.

"— that you could do with a bite or two, and that a well-made warming drink would not go amiss."

The Rat opened the door completely and looked at the contents of the Mole's basket with unabashed pleasure.

"Is it very bad, the news you have from the River?" said the Mole.

The Rat abruptly turned his attention from the basket to the Mole and his expression changed.

"I think it may be, Mole, for her call these past two days has been strange. She worries me. She worries me a great deal."

The Rat stood with his old friend, staring at the light of evening upon the River, and listening to the distant calls of the migrating geese, which had settled for the night in the nearby meadows.

Quietly Otter and Portly came to join them, and not long afterwards Nephew also arrived, for he had been worried about his uncle. Nephew sensed the importance of the occasion immediately and settled down with the others to contemplate the silent flow of the River.

For the time being all thought of food and drink had fled the Rat's mind, but a little later the Mole quietly

slipped into the Rat's house and made up a large pot of tea for the whole company. He brought it out, and while it brewed he opened up his basket and finally laid out some food for the Rat on a large plate.

The Water Rat took up the mug of tea the Mole had poured for him and sipped it slowly, hunching forward as he looked at the River, his hands tight about the mug as if for warmth and comfort.

"I cannot say that I fully understand what she has been trying to say to me since yesterday," he confided at last, "for the River does not use language as we do, but

13

speaks to us in a deeper way. Very often it is I who do
not understand her, but I think that on this occasion she
is not able to speak at all clearly of what concerns her.
It is as if she is calling for help, but . . . that she knows
we cannot give it. There! That's what it is: she needs
help, but not from us because there is nothing we can do
for her."

Ratty sounded suddenly relieved that his work
of communion had found expression after so many
arduous hours, but he sounded very tired as well.

"But what does she need our help *for*?" asked
Nephew, who had not yet learned, as his uncle had, that
on such occasions the Rat knew the questions well
enough; it was the answers that had to come in their
own time.

Yet perhaps because it *was* Nephew, of whom he had
grown very fond in the years since he had first come to
live with the Mole, the Rat did essay an answer.

"I do not know what it can be, but it's certain
it's important and threatens her very life and possibly
our own."

There was a gasp from Nephew and Portly, who had
been slower than the Mole and the Otter to understand
the sombre importance of what the Rat had been
saying, and they stared again at the great River whose
steady and relentless flow seemed as solid and eternal as
the cycle of day and night, and of the seasons.

"But how – ?" whispered Nephew.

"He doesn't know, he can't know," said the Otter,
replying for the Rat in a low voice, that animal having
now risen.

14

"Mole," the Rat called out when he had made his slow, tired way to his front door, "I'll be well and rested in a day or two and will come and see you then. Meanwhile, let us say no more of this amongst ourselves, or to Badger. I think it better that I talk to him myself about it first, for idle chatter on matters of moment is to nobody's advantage, least of all *hers*."

"Uncle," began Nephew an hour later, after the little group had dispersed and the two moles were nearing Mole End by the light of the stars, "this *is* a serious business, isn't it?"

His uncle had said hardly a word since they had crossed the Iron Bridge, and in the last quarter of an hour his pace had slowed, evidence that he was deep in thought. Now he stopped, sniffed appreciatively at the night air, and leaned upon a gate that led into one of the pasture fields.

"No doubt of it, Nephew, none whatsoever. Ratty isn't given to making things up, and he never makes light of River business. I cannot think what the matter can be, and nor shall I try, for in that department we must leave ourselves in the good hands of Ratty and Otter, and to some extent in Portly's as well, for he is coming along very well, very well indeed.

"Meanwhile, as Ratty said, 'idle chatter' will help nobody, and I shall desist from it. Now, did you succeed in stopping the rattle in the window, and easing the front door somewhat?"

"I did," said Nephew good-humouredly, the more so because such jobs were much easier without the house-proud Mole fussing about, and he had been glad that his uncle had followed his gentle hint and made himself scarce for the day.

"There's still a good deal of work to do on the other windows, however, and I will need your help holding the ladder on that highest window of all, which needs a good clean and rub-down, and then some fresh paint."

"Even more than that I fancy," said the Mole, "for I put in that window myself when I first came to Mole End, and that's a good many years ago – before you were born."

Talking in this comforting manner, they resumed the last stage of their journey, and once back in the security of Mole End they soon turned in. It had been a long day, and a worrying one, but the Mole always said that a good night's sleep cleared the mind and made things look different, and very often a good deal better; and often he was right.

If he had hoped for a lie-in, however, he was disappointed, for the sun seemed barely to have risen when there was a rat-tat-tat at the door.

"That must be Ratty!" he said, as he rose from his bed and searched for his dressing-gown. "He must have made a bit more sense of what the River was trying to tell him and come over at once to tell me."

Rat-tat-tat! went the knocker once more, rousing Nephew from his slumbers too.

Grumbling a little, and calling to Ratty to be patient *if* you please, the Mole slid back the bolts and finally opened the door.

"Ratty, you're always welcome," began the Mole,

"but do remember that not everybody is as wide awake at this hour as —"

But it was not the Rat. It was a solid gentleman in a blue and red uniform, and he carried a brown canvas satchel with a red crown upon it, above which were embroidered the words "Royal Mail".

The Mole saw at once the mistake the postman had made.

"It'll be Mr Toad of Toad Hall you want," he said, his normal good humour returning as he saw that the weather was fine and another good day seemed certain, "but I'm very much afraid you've come too far."

"I know where Mr Toad lives," said the postman slowly. "Everybody knows *him*. But I can't say as we've ever had to deliver further afield than his establishment, not in my experience and that goes back a good way now."

"Ah," said the Mole equably, feeling that in some way he may have called into question the postman's professionalism.

"You're Mr Mole of Mole End, I take it, seeing as you're mole-like and your house is named 'Mole End'?"

"That is correct," concurred the Mole.

"So you're not Mr Water Rat? And nor is *he*, I take it, since he, too, is mole-like?"

Nephew had appeared at the door behind the Mole and the postman was staring at him rather suspiciously.

"Neither of us is the Water Rat," said the Mole, feeling that simple agreement was the best approach with this gentleman.

"It's easier in the Town," said the postman wearily. "There's numbers on the houses there. If I had my way

I would have the law changed and get numbers put on every house in the land."

"I see," said the Mole, "but do you not feel that it would be pleasant to retain the house name as well?"

"Can't see the point," said the postman.

"No, I don't suppose you can," said the Mole.

"I can't stop here all day talking to you, now can I?" said the postman suddenly. "The letters of the land must be delivered – not to mention *other things*."

Mole glanced at his satchel, wondering if it might contain some of those "other things", and if so if they might be dangerous in some way. But the bag appeared to be empty, which was perhaps not surprising since Mole End was the last house in this direction for a great many miles.

"Would you like a cup of tea and some buttered toast?" offered the Mole, thinking that perhaps that was the way to deal with postmen.

"That is against all the regulations," said the postman with considerable severity, "and it is as well that you did not include with that invitation the suggestion – a hint would have been enough – that alcoholic beverage was included, or else I would have had to make a citizen's arrest and turn you and every other person resident in this house over to the magistrates."

"Well I –" began the perplexed Mole, who had never thought that the offer of sustenance to a visitor might land him in court.

"Don't you think, sir, that it would be better if you said nothing more on the subject of tea and toast? Instead, perhaps you could just try to give me a straight and unequivocal answer to a simple question: if Mr Rat does not live here, where does he live?"

"On the other side of the River," said the Mole, pointing down through the trees. "It's about half an hour or so if you go back the way you've come and over the Iron Bridge, but a good deal quicker by boat."

"Very droll," said the postman with a scowl. "We are not issued with boats."

"I could perhaps take the letter or package to Ratty myself, he is a good fr—"

"Sir, you have an unfortunate habit of saying the wrong thing: I would not repeat that suggestion if I were you, because purloining mail is deemed a criminal rather than a civil offence!"

The Mole was not a little affronted by the postman's attitude, but he was also most curious and intrigued, for to his certain knowledge the Rat had no more experience with the Royal Mail, in either the receiving or sending departments, than he had. He was reluctant to ask further questions, since he did indeed seem to say or ask the wrong thing and had not quite realized the risks attached to dealing with postmen, but quite suddenly the postman softened a little and offered some information.

"In any case," he said, "it isn't a letter."

"Not a letter," said the Mole, feeling that repetition of what was said to him was the safest approach.

"Nor a package."

"Ah," said the Mole. "Nor a package."

"Not even an 'Address Unknown Return To Sender'."

"Not even that!" exclaimed the Mole, feeling that he was beginning to get the hang of things.

"No, sir, we don't often get to deliver one of these, and seeing as it's caused me so much trouble I'm not sure I want to deliver another one."

He dug deep into the bag.

"What is it?" asked the Mole, quite forgetting himself.

But now the postman seemed willing enough to talk.

"This," he said, "is a Customer Instruction to Collect – that's on this side – and Customer Permission to Receive and Take Away – that's on *this* side. Collect from the Town Head Post Office, that is, seeing as the item is too big, or bulky, or in some other way not party to the normal regulations. Clearly we cannot as post-men undertake the risk to our persons of delivering such items, so the customer must take it upon himself."

The Mole saw at once that he had been quite correct to think that "other things" might be in some way dangerous. He permitted himself a momentary and uncharacteristic sense of selfish relief that it was not he who was to receive this Instruction to Collect, but the Rat. But then the Rat was more practical than he and would no doubt know what to do, or soon work it out.

"What is the nature of the item?" asked Nephew, as curious as his uncle.

"I am not permitted to tell you that," said the post-man, "but there is nothing to prevent me reading out what is upon the card, and nothing to prevent you hearing me do so."

He held up the card, squinted at it long and hard, and uttered a single and most startling word.

"Livestock," he said.

"I beg your pardon?" said the Mole.

"I shall endeavour to read out this word again, sir, and I trust you will endeavour to hear it this time."

He held up the card once more, peered at it, and uttered that astonishing word again, quite clearly, and for all to hear.

"Livestock," said he.

"And Mr Rat is to collect it?"

"Or them, sir; you never can tell with livestock."

"Are you permitted to read anything else on the card which may give us a clue about this matter?" continued the Mole, his curiosity undeniable.

"The only other item that may have relevance, sir – and beyond this I know nothing myself, for incoming mail and other items is a different department, of course – concerns the *source* of said item. That often gives a clue. For example, if the source were 'The Cheesery, Wensleydale, Yorkshire', you might reasonably conclude it was a Wensleydale cheese."

"But that wouldn't be livestock," said the Mole.

"I would not be quite so sure upon that point, sir, if I were you, given some of the cheeses I have seen lingering in the Sorting Office."

"So with respect to livestock, if the source were something such as a farm, for example, or – ?"

"Or an abattoir, sir, in those cases where said livestock is no longer alive, or in other words is dead. But in this case –"

"Yes?" said the Mole eagerly.

"– the source *is* quoted, and again I must remind you that –"

"Yes, yes," said the Mole impatiently, having now got the measure of this postman and seeing that he was as curious about the matter as the Mole himself.

"Well then, the source is given as 'Egypt'!" said the postman without further ado.

"O my!" said the Mole, whose knowledge of Egyptian livestock was restricted to camels. "O my!"

"A sentiment with which I wholeheartedly agree, sir."

At which the Mole suggested that he and Nephew guide the postman to the Rat without more delay by way of the River.

The walk down to the bank was pleasant, and confirmed the promise of the dawn, and as the Mole had expected, the Rat was already out on his side of the River, busying himself about his boat and moorings.

"Mole! Good, good. Just the fellow I was hoping to see —"

He stopped the moment he saw the postman, with a look of surprise and enquiry on his face. The matter was very soon explained, however, if not yet understood. Over came the Rat in his boat in a trice, but as the postman refused to hand the item to him directly and insisted he must deliver it personally to the Water Rat's address, back over the River they all went.

"It must be a mistake," said the Rat finally, when the card had been read several times and the matter had been fully explained to him. "I know nobody in Egypt, and I have certainly not ordered any camels."

"It can't be helped, I'm afraid, sir: rules are rules. We, that is the Royal Mail, assumed responsibility for this item the moment it touched the shores of the land, but you took up that same responsibility once you had acknowledged receipt, if only mutely, which is to say through silent reading of the card. Then, allowing for a day's grace once you are informed of said livestock's presence, you must pay storage charges at a rate of sixpence a day minimum. Herds work out more dearly than individuals."

"Well –" said the Rat.

"Be warned, sir, those charges soon mount up. In the case of Lord Bell, former cotton king of Glasgow, who foolishly acknowledged receipt of fifteen gross bales of cotton from India but omitted to collect them for six years, the charges bankrupted him, and he went to gaol!"

"O dear, Ratty, you had better collect it today," said the Mole.

"But the last thing I want on a day like this is to go to the Town!"

24

"In a case such as yours, sir," advised the postman, who was used to difficult customers and knew how to spot their weak points, "the first item the bailiffs would take, as part payment of unpaid charges, would certainly be that boat of yours."

"Not my boat!" said the horrified Rat, eyeing the craft that had given him and the Mole so much happiness, and which had been so damaged on some of their more dangerous expeditions that it had taken all his skills and patience to restore it.

"And the oars, sir. They'd have to go as well. If you take my advice you'll collect this item forthwith."

"Yes, I will, I *must*," said a very subdued Ratty. "But, Mole?"

"Yes?"

"Perhaps you'd come with me, and Nephew too, for if this livestock proves to be a herd of something rather than a single specimen then I shall need a good deal of help."

He sighed, and looked about the River with considerable misgiving, for the morning was turning glorious, and a journey to the Town was never to his taste, particularly on so promising a day as this and with the River's warning of yesterday still so much on his mind.

"It will take me a good deal more than a day to get there in my boat," said the Rat, "for I shall have to row all the way. There's nothing for it but to borrow Toad's motor-launch."

Having escorted the postman to the Iron Bridge and said their farewells, and with the collection card carefully stowed away in Rat's inside pocket, they marched purposefully up to Toad Hall to see if they might borrow Toad's launch for the day.

It had been some time since any of them had seen Toad. They found him in the great hall by his front door studying a good many packing cases of all shapes and sizes of which he had evidently recently taken delivery. They all had upon them the imprint of the Town's best-known emporium for the better classes and, stencilled in black, the words: IMMEDIATE DELIVERY.

Toad's greeting, normally so effusive and generous-hearted, was on this occasion subdued. He was sitting in a chair, eyeing the cases as if he were summoning up the energy and courage to open them.

"O, hullo!" he said in a preoccupied way.

"Anything we can help with, old fellow?" offered the practical Rat.

"I am afraid not," said Toad.

"Is this, perhaps, some new equipment for your home?" suggested the Mole, his curiosity getting the better of him.

"My home? No," muttered Toad, "nor even for me."

Then he rose up, paced about, sighed a good deal and said, "But what's the use of talking to you fellows, who have no real responsibilities except towards yourselves, whereas I have parental duties to consider, and much else to worry about? Now what can I do for you?"

It was plain that Toad did not wish to be pressed further, so the Rat quickly explained why they so much needed to borrow his launch. Toad was only too happy to oblige, for whatever else one might say about Toad of Toad Hall, he was never mean with his possessions. But as for going with them . . .

"Much as I would like to, you fellows really must try to understand that I have a good deal to attend to today, and much to worry about, so very much! You go off and have a good time, but if you have a moment to spare a thought for me, please do so. You see, in addition to this delivery I have to deal with, *he's* coming home today."

"Ah!" exclaimed the Mole. "I quite forgot; so he is."

"Who?" enquired the puzzled Rat.

"Master Toad," said the Mole quietly.

"Ah! Yes, well, we'd best be on our way," said the Rat hastily, adding with not entirely convincing regret, "but you're definitely not able to come with us?"

"You'll just have to do your very best to have a good time without me," said Toad, showing them out onto the terrace. "You know where my craft is, Ratty, and how it works, just as well as I do; better in fact! Now off you go, for I have so much to do!"

With that he dashed inside as the others made their way down to his boat-house. In no time at all the Rat had the motor-launch out on the River, and had turned it expertly upstream towards the Town; while behind them, though the River Bank was aflame with autumn sun, the River itself was still and sombre, its surface seeming already to reflect the dark hues of approaching winter.

· II ·
Master Toad

What so preoccupied Toad that day was the same matter that had preoccupied him daily and weekly in the years since he had assumed guardianship of his distant relative, the Count d'Albert-Chapelle, and accepted the spoilt youth into his house and home.

The once carefree Toad, who for most of his life had only himself to think about, was now in a nearly constant state of worry and concern about his youthful kin, whose return from a Grand Tour of the Continent was expected at any moment.

He was no longer called "The Count" along the River Bank, however, except occasionally by Toad when he was eager to impress somebody with the nobility of his family and connections. No, those who lived thereabouts, such as Mole and Rat, Otter and Badger, had taken to referring to Toad's ward simply as "Master Toad". This was partly to distinguish him in conversation from Toad himself, but also because as a name and description it fitted him rather well.

At first the Count had been very happy with this, for his English was not then good enough to understand the difference between "Master" in a youthful sense and "Maestro" in its more Continental and authoritative sense, and the toad in him naturally inclined to the latter interpretation.

Most unfortunately, somebody had put him right on the point a year or so after his arrival at Toad Hall. At the time he had been passing through an especially bad stage of the irritating physical and emotional changes that beset those caught between youth and adulthood, and had taken to carrying a silver-topped cane and wearing those outlandish garments so favoured by indulged youths of the privileged classes. He therefore stood upon his dignity and insisted that people should begin calling him "Count".

The wise Badger advised everybody to accede to Master Toad's demands at once, and call him "Count" just as he asked, but with very special emphasis and deference every time they used it. Sure enough, it was not long before this began to vex the youth greatly. He had come to like the River Bank and its inhabitants very much, since they comprised the first real home he had had, and being no fool he soon saw the absurdity of putting on airs and graces among those who had come to know him so well and like him as he was.

"Please," he said, after only a few days, "I would, after all, prefer it if you would call me Master Toad like you always 'ave."

It must be said at this point that it was much to Master Toad's credit that he quickly realized that the better he spoke English, the better it was for him. He still had difficulty remembering his "aitches" but, except for moments of stress or emotional excitement, when he would break back into French, and when attempting some of the more complex Anglo-Saxon constructions, he was beginning to be able to pass himself off as an Englishman.

In this endeavour he was greatly helped by Toad's decision to send him to one of the leading public schools – indeed, some might say the very best. At first Toad's friends had resisted this idea, but as time passed and the youth grew more difficult and extreme in some of his eccentricities, it had begun to make a good deal of sense.

Certainly the boarding school to which Master Toad was sent, which lies within the very shadow of the Monarch's home, was the most expensive in the land, but then this mattered not one whit to Toad, who, now that the expenses of re-building Toad Hall following the fire that gutted it some years before had been defrayed, had a good deal of disposable income once again. What was a fortune to other animals upon the River Bank was no more than an incidental expense to Toad.

Master Toad himself had nothing but his name, for the family fortunes in France had been lost by his late father the Count, who had been both gullible and over-optimistic in business matters, a fatal combination. Such funds as remained went the mother's way, and since she was now re-married and living in Australia with Toad's former butler, it was unlikely that Master Toad would gain very much financial support from her. But no matter, Toad did not care one bit, and begrudged not a single penny he lavished upon his ward, just as he never for one moment counted the cost in any of his acts of generosity to others and indulgence to himself.

Most unfortunately, Master Toad had discovered that money − Toad's money − buys friends, or at least acquaintances, of a kind that were a generally baleful influence upon him. Yet his popularity was not due only to his wealth − indeed there were a number of fellow pupils whose paters were a good deal more wealthy than Toad, and in certain respects much better connected: namely, the sons of the High Judge (whom Toad had met occasionally in a professional capacity), the Commissioner of Police (another professional acquaintance of Toad's) and that Bishop whom Toad had previously known as "Senior", but who had very recently been promoted "Most Senior Bishop".

Master Toad had had to earn the respect and loyalty of these three the hard way, and he had done so splendidly. He was better than his schoolmates at muddy games, and at avoiding those they did not wish to play, he was a good deal more imaginative in thinking up new japes and pranks, and he showed considerably more flair and courage in the execution of the same.

In some respects Master Toad became their leader, and it was undoubtedly from him that they gained the title that gave them such notoriety as a group, for they were known as the Four Musketeers. It is said that to this day that educational establishment still bears the scars of their activities.

For example: in the form of water-stains on dormitory ceilings from flooding caused by the removal of ballcocks from attic plumbing; smoke marks in two senior common rooms and the Master's Hall from their blocking up of a suite of chimneys with a consignment of rugby balls; and, most notorious of all and a cause of a term's rustication for each of them, the hiring of some navvies (who should have known better) to demolish a large part of that ancient wall against which the school's most hallowed game had long been played, and the re-use of its stones, bricks, flints and cement for a soup-kitchen then being built for vagrants, waifs and strays.

It was following this incident, with which Master Toad declared himself exceptionally pleased, that all Four Musketeers descended upon Toad Hall together, and had a great deal of fun at the expense of Toad and his friends.

The issuing of free liquor to all the weasels and stoats was perhaps forgivable, as were other pranks: upon the Mole (an order for one hundred bottles of his sloe and blackberry drink, ostensibly from the most prestigious store in the Town, which had the Mole in a flap for several days); upon the Rat (a seemingly legitimate requisition by the Royal Navy of his much-loved boat for active service against the Nordic Kingdoms in retaliation for their sacking of Lindisfarne in AD 793, which caused poor Ratty considerable anguish); and upon the Badger (an apparently genuine request from the editor of that most august daily organ, *The Times*, to contribute a regular column upon country matters, the first of which he worked upon very hard indeed, only to receive a rejection slip as false and mischievous as the original request, accompanied by the comment "should try harder, or not at all").

On the whole, the River Bank's inhabitants were big-hearted and good-humoured enough to tolerate such jokes, provided they were not too frequent, but then Master Toad and his friends went a little too far. Making mock of the adult world they were so soon to join was one thing, attempting to divert the River into the Canal quite another. They preceded this folly by sending Official Notices to all those living along its banks to expect "the River to cease its flow with effect from next Sunday, 9.00 AM prompt." Yes, that was beyond a joke, and might have had long-lasting consequences had not the Rat and the Otter taken urgent corrective action.

A deputation led by the Badger called upon Toad and persuaded him to discipline his ward, and send his fellow pranksters packing. This he had duly done, and peace had returned to the River Bank once more (for the time being). The youth had returned to his educational establishment for the summer term, and Toad had thoughtfully arranged for him to take a Grand Tour of several European capitals in the holiday weeks thereafter, which had put the River Bank back onto an even keel for the summer months.

Now that respite was over, however, and with the final academic year before the youth was thrust out upon the world about to begin, Master Toad was expected to return to Toad Hall for some cramming in vital subjects before the new term commenced.

In all these circumstances, it is little wonder that the Rat and his friends had found Toad in such a dither of worry and concern. The Mole might very well have been annoyed with himself for not remembering about Master Toad's return, for he had been party to its planning a month previously.

"When Master Toad goes away he always comes back changed for the worse in some way," Toad had complained to him as they took tea together. "You see, Mole, either he won't talk to me, or he is vain and conceited in a way that is quite unpardonable and really quite uncharacteristic of our family – I might say our noble family, which certainly has a good deal to be vain and conceited about, but normally has the politeness not to show it!"

"Yes, Toad," said the compliant Mole, who had shared with the Badger and the others a certain amusement in watching Toad's battles with his ward, and enjoyed the irony of watching an arch-poacher in the department of vanity and conceit struggling to turn gamekeeper.

"I don't believe he'll ever improve," groaned Toad, "or show the slightest consideration for others. Now he is to be here till school starts again. What am I to do with him?"

"And yet, Toad, when it comes down to it, you do like having him about the place, don't you?"

Toad thought for only a very few moments before, as impulsive and generous in spirit as ever, he cried, "Yes, I like him being here, I suppose – I really do! He adds life to the Hall, and has a knack of getting his way with the staff that reminds me of when I was young and without responsibility. I do not think he's bad at heart, you know. It's just . . . well, it's that –"

"Yes, Toad?" murmured the Mole.

"O, well, I shall say it: when he's here I am miserable and when he is not here I am even more miserable. I miss him very much when he is away at school, and this summer all I have had from him are two postcards, from Baden-Baden and Venice respectively, depicting fat ladies and thin gentlemen uttering what he facetiously calls *double entendres,* and –"

"Two postcards are better than none, Toad," offered the Mole truthfully.

"– and unpaid bills from Berlin, Prague, Madrid, Cannes, Biarritz, Naples and Casablanca, the nature of the last of which gave me great cause for concern!"

The Mole had laughed gently, for if Master Toad did nothing else – though in fact he did a great deal more, and the Mole saw much in the youth that Toad ought to be thankful for – he provided them all with a good deal to think and talk about.

"O, I know he can be reasonable sometimes," Toad had continued. "He can be lovable, he can even be thoughtful if he puts his mind to it, but what stress and heartache he causes me! I believe I have aged ten years for every year he has been with me."

There was some truth in this, though the Mole told himself that Master Toad could hardly be blamed for that. Toad had put on a good deal of weight, and huffed and puffed more than he used to when he exerted himself, which was not often. He also had difficulty in reading small print these days and had had spectacles prescribed, which he occasionally used when he thought nobody was looking.

"We are all getting older," said the Mole companionably.

And there was truth in this too, for the years had come and they had gone along the River Bank, and time had taken its toll upon them all. The Water Rat, for example, was increasingly irritable these days, especially if things were not just as he liked them, and he often seemed tired and distracted, quite worryingly so, in Mole's opinion.

The Badger, for his part, had begun to grow deaf, and all of them had difficulty at times being understood by him, except Grandson, who lived with him now. He had developed the knack of raising his voice without losing his intonation, in such a way that the Badger understood everything he said.

Nor was the Otter quite the animal he had been, for he swam more slowly than before, and his sight under water was not at all what it had been. Why, these days, Portly – now no longer quite as tubby as he had been when he gained his nickname – was better at catching fish than his own father!

Of them all perhaps the Mole seemed least affected by age, though he suffered aches and pains most mornings, and those injuries he had sustained some years previously at the jaws of the Lathbury Pike, when only his courage against that lethal foe had saved the Rat's life, gave him trouble when atmospheric pressure rose and the wind veered to the north and turned chill.

"It will all work out for the best in the end, Toad," the Mole had said at the end of their discussion.

"I hope so," said Toad, "but meanwhile I have arranged for a motor-car manned with some reliable former constables to meet Master Toad off the boat and ensure he comes straight home without a repetition of what happened last time."

"Ah, you mean when he came to Toad Hall from Dover by way of a spot of motor-cycle racing on the Isle of Man?"

"There will be no repeat of that kind of thing when he comes home this time!" said Toad. "None whatsoever!"

"No, Toad," said the Mole.

"And what is more he will work at his school books in my study every day till three o'clock in the afternoon, after which I shall take him out myself for some light educational exercise and then pack him off early to bed."

"Yes, Toad."

So it was that in this startling way, and in a very much shorter period than it had taken the combined efforts of the Badger, Rat, Otter and Mole, working on the same project and achieving something little better than complete failure, Master Toad's presence on the River Bank had reformed Toad into a responsible, care-worn pater, much like any other. One, indeed, no longer capable of leaping aboard his own craft and guiding them all to the Town in the wild and irresponsible way that had always been his wont; but rather, one who must stay at home and fret and worry.

"I rather miss the old Toad," observed the Mole that same day as he, the Rat and Nephew left Toad's estate behind and headed towards the Town in the motor-launch.

"Do you know, old chap, now you mention it, I believe I do myself," confided the Rat. "I would rather like to see Toad getting up to his old tricks one last time!"

"Just what I was trying to say!" cried the Mole, quite forgetting that Nephew was there and ought not to hear such things. "Why, in his younger days he was capable of pranks very much worse than any Master Toad has ever got up to − *far* worse, now I come to think of it."

"Do you remember that time he stole a motor-car?"

The Rat might very well have continued with this oft-told tale, but they were at that part of the journey when the River ran quite close to the new road lately opened up between the Town and the River Bank, and his voice was suddenly drowned out by the rapid passage of a motor-car, horns blaring, accompanied by a loud, braying laughter that sounded dreadfully familiar.

"Toad?" whispered the Mole, as if he had heard a ghost.

"Toad?" gasped the Rat, as if he had seen one.

"*Master* Toad," observed Nephew matter-of-factly, "probably."

"But −" began the Mole, standing on tiptoe to catch a glimpse of the motor-car as it rushed by, "but Toad quite specifically arranged −"

"Think no more of it. Say nothing more of it. Do nothing about it," said the Rat. "We are about important business and cannot, must not, be diverted from our purpose. Nephew, stop trying to see that motor-car, the road is out of view from here and it will have reached Toad Hall by now at the speed it was going! Concentrate on . . . drat!"

The diversion caused by Master Toad had quite distracted the normally masterful Rat, and but for Nephew's liberal use of a boathook, and the Mole's dabbling with an oar, they would certainly have hit the bank rather harder than they did.

"Humph!" exclaimed the Rat, getting them back on course. "No more conversation amongst the crew, if you don't mind!"

"Uncle, did you see?" whispered Nephew a little later.

The Mole nodded with resignation, and told Nephew to say no more about it, the Rat was already in a bad enough mood as it was.

Of course he had seen, seen all too clearly: a gentleman of large and stocky build in the front passenger seat of the motor-car, gagged and bound. And in the rear two more, clearly dealt with in the same way. While in the driver's seat, scarf flying, laughing and behaving in a manner that was entirely reprehensible, was a toad who looked very much as Toad used to look in days gone by, when he was enjoying himself at other people's expense.

"But, Pater," which is what Master Toad called his guardian when he knew he had gone too far and felt that a show of respect might not go amiss, "had you only *told* me that the gentleman who claimed to be in your employ had been sent by you to Dover to see me safely home, and not to abduct me and demand a large ransom for my safe return, which is the impression he very soon gave, then *of course* I would not have treated him as I did.

"But I must say that my suspicions regarding his claim to be a former policeman of considerable experience were very amply confirmed when he allowed himself to be bound with his own handcuffs and gagged with his own handkerchief. I know how you detest constables, along with lawyers, churchmen and others who generally seek to curb our liberties, and I could not imagine for one moment you would employ one, let alone three. Really I cannot be blamed for anything that happened!"

Toad did not for one moment believe a word of this nonsense, but then the ex-constable had not made his case easier by being duped by a mere youth. Toad knew perfectly well that he would have tried the same trick, and that he would have felt as smug as Master Toad now looked if he had pulled it off.

Yet Toad was not entirely down-hearted by the nature of his ward's arrival, for whatever the rights and wrongs of the affair it gave him an early opportunity to lay down the law regarding duties and responsibilities, much as he had outlined them to the Mole some weeks before. To his surprise and relief Master Toad did not raise any objections, rather the opposite in fact, for he claimed to be very eager to get on with some school-work, and overjoyed to have a timetable to follow, and strict meal times to observe.

"I am in need of improvement," said Master Toad piously, "for I 'ave wasted my schooldays in laziness and foolishness and now I must work and be good."

Toad could scarcely believe his ears – indeed he did *not* believe his ears, and concluded that far from knocking some sense into the youth, the Grand Tour had encouraged him towards a high level of accomplishment in acting, which might, if all else failed, help Master Toad find ready employment upon the stage.

"When did you come to realize the errors of your ways?" asked the suspicious Toad.

"It was when I was in Rome at confession after 'oly Communion in St Paul's Cathedral. I see a light, I hear a voice saying, 'Henri, be good, study 'ard,' and I confess my sins to the padre."

"St *Paul's* you say?" said Toad evenly.

"Exactement!" came the reply, and the over-confident embellishment gave the game away, "I 'ave seen the name upon a board outside: 'St Paul's, the Pope's Own Church.' 'Ave you been to Rome, Monsieur Toad?"

"As a matter of fact, I have – my father sent me at about your age, for much the same reason, and with about the same effect. In those days the cathedral was called St Peter's, but perhaps –"

"So many impressions, so many places, so easy to confuse," said Master Toad airily, affecting not to notice that his cathedral visit had been exposed as fraudulent, but in truth considerably discomforted.

"All the more reason to work hard at your books," said the ruthless Toad, who felt very pleased with himself at having so easily demonstrated who held the whip hand in the Hall. "Now, you have time for at least two hours' work before teatime!"

Whether or not Master Toad really used the next two

hours for work mattered not a bit to Toad; he was
quiet and he was obedient, and up in his room he was,
relatively speaking, out of harm's way.

Later, over tea, the two began chatting again, and very
soon Toad was thoroughly enjoying an engaging
account of the trials and tribulations, the triumphs and
the disasters, such as any young person, journeying
about the Continent, albeit first class and via the best
hotels, is likely to experience.

Finally, matters came round to the River Bank, and
Toad was gratified that his young friend showed rather
more interest in the doings of the Mole and the others
than he had earlier in the year, and even expressed a
desire to see his friend, Mole's Nephew, at the earliest
opportunity.

"I hope there will be no objection, when my work is
done, if I borrow the motor-launch —"

"There is every objection," said Toad, happy that he
had foreseen this request and, having considered the
dangers inherent in granting such permission, had
decided that a total veto was the best policy. "In any
case," he added, "Ratty and Mole are themselves using
it just now, so it is not even here."

"Aah . . . and what about that motor-car that gave me
such a pleasing journey from Dover?"

"Rented," said Toad shortly, "and already on its way
back to Dover. The former constable has taken it, along
with his incompetent colleagues."

"Aah . . . " said the defeated youth.

Toad rather expected some complaints at this point
but Master Toad made none. Rather, he asked in a sweet

and winning way what "educational exercise" Toad had in mind for the following afternoon.

Toad rose from the chaise longue in which he normally took tea and paced busily about the conservatory. He was rather excited about the exercise he had organized, and a trifle nervous too, for it was not something he had often engaged in if he could possibly avoid it. But just lately this particularly activity had come into fashion and Toad was not one to be left behind. More to the point, every expert lecturer and author upon the subject (he had been to several lantern slides and cinematograph lectures, and had acquired a large quantity of helpful books, which he was hoping shortly to find time to read) made the point that this pursuit was especially healthy and educational for its followers.

"Pater, what is the exercise to be?" repeated his ward.

"We shall be going hiking," said Toad, with as much enthusiasm and confidence as he could muster.

"'iking?" repeated Master Toad in some considerable surprise. He thought he knew what the word meant, but he could not connect it with his guardian.

"Hiking during the week, and cycling at weekends," said Toad, weakening a little, for the cycling was a reserve activity for which he had little relish. The last time he had been upon a bicycle he had been pursued by His Lordship's pack of hounds, who had caused him to crash headlong into a hedge and might have devoured him (as he recalled it) had he not fought them off with his bare hands.

He had decided, however, that a guardian must suffer in the course of his duties, and along with the two sets of walking gear he had ordered from a prestigious department store in the Town, which prided itself on supplying anything to anybody anywhere, even in the furthest-flung part of the Empire, he had also ordered two gentleman's cycles.

"But hiking's the thing," said Toad. "The most exciting and ennobling form of exploration there is!"

"*Le* 'iking is exploring without the convenience of 'orse, motor-car, train, omnibus, bicycle, or any other way of transporting one person or more from 'ere to . . . there, *non*?" suggested Master Toad with very considerable distaste, gazing down with enormous sadness at the ground beneath him. "*Le* 'iking is on the feet only, yes?"

"Hiking," said Toad, who was pleased that his ward understood at least the rudiments, and not displeased that he saw this new pastime as a challenge, for he believed that to be effective educational exercise would have in some way to be hard and strenuous, "hiking, I believe, is really the only way to get about and see things. When I was younger I foolishly thought that, say, a caravan might —"

"O, yes, *monsieur*!" exclaimed Master Toad, who not five minutes before would have refused to go anywhere near a caravan.

"And then I was seduced, that is not too strong a word for it, by motor-cars —"

"Yes, they are wonderful, so perhaps —"

"Then I settled upon an aeronautical future for myself, and —"

"Pater, I wished very much to 'ave a word with you about flying lessons, because —"

47

"But none of them offers the same combination of healthy exertion, freedom of choice and demands upon the character and intelligence as hiking."

"You 'ave done this 'iking before, then?" asked Master Toad softly.

Toad had never in his life willingly hiked anywhere, to his knowledge. On those few occasions when he had found himself in wild parts without some form of conveyance, usually when a fugitive from the law, he had devoted his considerable enterprise to getting back to normality as quickly as he possibly could, and into a comfortable chair at home.

Except . . . now he thought of it, there *had* been an occasion, lasting many weeks, when Toad had wandered free across the land, weeks which he could barely now remember, though there were remnants of them still in his fickle and errant memory, when he had woken up under hedgerows, shared meals by the fires of friendly itinerants, and gone to sleep hungry by the light of the stars.

That episode had occurred after his release from one of his sojourns in gaol when, for reasons best forgotten, he did not feel able to show his face about the River Bank for a time. Now it was all coming back to him, and he saw it had not been all bad.

"Yes," said Toad simply and truthfully, "I *have* hiked as it happens, which I can see surprises you considerably. Not much, it is true, but enough to know the truth of what I say about this excellent pursuit. Therefore, young sir, we shall hike at least five days a week, and if you refuse or resist or fail to look anything but pleased and delighted with this pastime, I shall —"

"Yes, Monsieur?" said Master Toad with the easy insolence of one who does not believe for one moment that his pater will do anything at all to harm him.

"– I have decided that I shall no longer pay your school fees and that you must go forthwith to work!"

Toad had never offered any real sanction to the youth before and was rather surprised to find himself doing so now, but there had been such an irritating confidence in the way that "Yes, Monsieur?" had been uttered that a new resolution to be firm and severe had come over him.

"O *non!*" cried the youth, staring up in considerable dismay. "Not real work – with my hands!"

Master Toad recognized that there was a new tone in Toad's voice. He had been much looking forward to going back to school where all his friends were, but now . . . O, how horrible Toad Hall was! How terrible his guardian was!

"Well?" said Toad.

"I shall be so 'appy to 'ike every afternoon before tea," said the youth compliantly, though, in truth, he was already planning how he might evade in every way possible this most loathsome and humiliating of pastimes.

"And now," said Toad equably, recognizing that look in the youth's narrowed eyes very well, for he had looked thus at his father years ago, "you have an hour before you need to change for dinner. Badger is coming, and Mole, Ratty and Otter if they are back from their journey to the Town. You know how stimulating you find their company."

"Yes," agreed Master Toad reluctantly, doing his best

to put a brave face on it. "But Nephew and Portly – do they not come?"

Toad smiled broadly and put an affectionate hand upon his ward's shoulder, for he felt he had gone far enough.

"Don't worry. They are all coming. I would not be so heartless as to impose my old friends upon you without asking along some of your own. They have greatly missed you this summer, and they want to hear all about your adventures and misadventures upon the Continent."

For the first time since his return, Master Toad grinned. He went back to his books with renewed vigour, quite forgetting the passionate dislike of Toad he had felt only moments before, but feeling instead that it was perhaps good, after all, to be home.

· III ·
Livestock

The Mole and Water Rat had last journeyed up-river together to the Town several years previously, at the time of their renowned expedition, when they had explored the dangerous and little-known upper reaches of that tributary which forms the western boundary of His Lordship's estate.

They had ventured up the tributary on that occasion only after turning back from the Town when they had seen enough of its chimneys, factories, traffic and busy people, and decided such a route was not for them. They did not regret their decision, even though their journey led to a near-fatal encounter with the Lathbury

Pike, which had so grievously injured the Mole, and had brought their expedition to a summary end.

Now, as they passed the entrance to the tributary once more, they paused awhile and told Nephew something of their adventures there, before proceeding past that part of the riverbank owned by His Lordship. They could not but notice that a good many changes, all for the worse, had taken place.

For one thing, His Lordship appeared to have shored up his bank with concrete and built a new jetty, so that it looked less natural, and less pleasing than they remembered it. For another, it was all too clear that a good deal more building had taken place along the River's banks, so that the Town was now considerably extended. Yet not, as they might have hoped, with pleasing villas and riverside houses of the kind exemplified by His Lordship's House and, on a smaller scale, by Toad Hall.

There were a few tawdry attempts at fine houses such as these, but they were in red brick, and their frontages were quite spoilt by signs that said "No Fishing Here" and "Trespassers Will Be Prosecuted", and even, in one case, the ominous words "Patrolled by Dogs, Day and Night".

Far worse, to the Mole and the Rat, was the growth in the number of industrial jetties and noisome factories whose chimneys belched out noxious fumes. On their last visit they had seen a few such buildings going up. Now they had to press on past a whole succession of factories, and pass much nearer than they would have wished to pipes pumping out waste fluids and foaming mess into the River.

"No wonder this vegetation looks all stunted and deformed!" exclaimed the Mole. "Give me the River Bank any day!"

The Rat, however, could only stand and stare, appalled at what he saw, and seemingly struck dumb by the way in which the River, *his* River, could be so ill-used.

"No wonder," he whispered finally, "no wonder I sensed the River's distress. Such waste and pollution are poisoning her, and this is surely what she has been trying to tell me. I must try to come back here soon with Otter to find out just how badly she is suffering."

Then, with a rueful shake of his head, he left behind the last riverside vegetation, powering their craft amongst endless jetties and oily backwaters, and past towering smoke-stained quays and walls, till they found a place to tie up.

Neither the Mole nor Nephew had ever been so far into the Town, and were quite dazed by the noise and confusion of the place. The Rat was made of sterner stuff, however. Business had brought him here from time to time over the years, but even he had difficulty following the directions they were given – more than once – to the Town's Head General Post Office.

Fortunately it was not located too far from the River. Yet how vast it seemed when they finally found it. On every side carts and conveyances of all kinds bearing the red and gold of the Royal Mail, filled to overflowing with bulging mailbags, arrived and departed, accompanied by the shouts and cries of those who loaded and unloaded them.

After a good many fruitless enquiries they eventually discovered that "Livestock" was located in a Special Department, far away from the regular items of mail. They negotiated their way down a side road, over two footbridges, behind a railway station and by way of an evil-smelling alley, till with some relief they spied a metal door above which projected an enamelled sign, which read, "Royal Mail, Livestock and Incidentals."

Looking at the small door, the Mole felt a little more cheerful and observed, "Well, Ratty, it's obvious that no herds of camels or elephants can pass in and out of here, so we may take heart."

Just then there was a mighty bellowing and a rumbling in the lane and buildings all about, such as four and twenty thousand stampeding oxen might make. Then they realized that what they thought were walls next to the door were in fact mighty iron-clad gates, which now shook and clattered, and seemed about to burst open to let the rampant herd inside escape.

"This small door is for us," said the Rat gloomily, "and I fear those great gates are for whatever it is we are to collect."

Considerably abashed, they passed through the door and the Rat presented his card to the thin, bespectacled gentleman who eventually answered their summons.

"Ah, yes," he said, peering at the card.

"Is it – or are they – large?" asked the Rat in trepidation.

"Large is a very relative word in this game," the Post Office official said. "For example, a cow is large relative to a sheep, is it not?"

"Yes," agreed the Rat, "but –"

"Whereas relative to some bulls, I can assure you that a cow will seem quite small."

"I see," said the Rat, "now —"

"But if you're talking large relative to *large,* then in my experience the largest we've had here is two white rhinoceroses for the Zoo. They *was* large, and one more than he should have been, since somehow or other en route to the Town, probably off the Liberian coast, he managed to get himself in the family way."

"You mean the rhinoceros was a female and —"

"We felt it wisest not to say so, sir, for that would have made the documents all wrong and he would have had to be sent back. There's no knowing the difficulties that would have ensued had we reclassified him as being of the female gender."

"But in our case?" said the Rat, striving to get back to the point.

"In your case, I am not permitted to comment upon size, gender or number, as it's cash on delivery, and a client's business is private."

"But is it camels?" persisted the Rat, who had decided that if it was, he would not accept delivery and hang the consequences.

"I can say it is not camels, sir, without breaking rules, because camels are stored down the lane where the buildings are taller, or rather have no roofs. Those buildings are in fact open space. Now, if you would just sign here, please, sir, and pay one farthing for the receipt stamp."

"Is that all? I thought I would have to pay much more than that!"

"I said cash on delivery and in a manner of speaking that is correct. But it came with the cash attached and I have taken the liberty of taking said amount, leaving you with a profit of sixpence three farthings, which is a unique occurrence in the C.O.D. department. Congratulations! There! That's done! Now, if you'll follow me, gentlemen, you can take delivery."

They passed through a succession of vast rooms lined with a great many cages and pens, filled with innumerable varieties of animals. It cannot be said that all the odours of these rooms and pens were pleasant, and not every sight that met their eyes was a delight. But the overwhelming feature was the sound, an endless cacophony of grunts and bellows (from the oxen they had heard before), hissing (from a consignment of Indian vipers) and bubbling (from several tanks of Chinese carp), moos and baas (from more familiar cattle and sheep) and the avian sounds of hoopoes and giant cockatoos, and the chatter, fortunately in Malay, of a gross of green parrots.

Every now and then the Rat or the Mole would stop and say, "Is it this?" or "Surely not that?" but always the Post Office official would urge them on.

"Not far now, just through the next two buildings!"

Finally, they reached the most dilapidated building they had yet come across.

"There's mainly pigs here," said the official, "but you'll find your item beyond them: number 2467 D. Be sure not to mix it up with the 2467 A & B, which are Peruvian goats, nor 2467 C, which I believe to be iguanas from the Galapagos Islands, though I can't be sure as they've gone to ground in the hay. This is the key to its cage, sir, so perhaps you could go and consider if you'll accept it, while I attend to some other business. I'll be with you by and by."

With that he was gone, and they made their way past aisle after aisle of grunting pigs to where their item awaited them. The cages were well labelled, A through to D, and the Peruvian goats were plain to see, and to smell as well. In C they saw a good deal of hay, and protruding from the bottom two reptilian tails.

Finally they came to cage D, which was somewhat in the shadows, since the only window at this end of the building was above the goats. At first it was hard to make out much at all, but as they grew accustomed to the gloom, they could make out the form of a living thing in the furthest corner of the cage – and then two bright eyes. Eyes that stared at them unblinkingly.

The creature was draped – dressed is too precise a word – with yards of a fabric that had long ago ceased to be white, and wore upon its head a curious hat, little more than a roundel of rags.

"What on earth is it?" said Nephew, speaking for them all.

"It is . . . " began the Mole, not at all sure he knew. "That is, it might be –"
But the Rat knew what it was the moment he saw it, though he could not imagine why it had been sent to him.

He knew what it was, and he was horror-struck.

58

"It is a rat," he said.

"A young rat," said the Mole.

"The most strangely dressed rat I ever saw," said Nephew. "As if . . . as if . . . "

"As if it has come from Egypt and is used to hot sunshine," continued the Mole.

The Water Rat, ever practical, unlocked the cage door.

The rat did not move, but only stared. Then, as if from very long habit, it tugged at some twine tied about its right wrist, to which was attached a large Royal Mail C.O.D. label, stamped *Paid*, upon which were several red-wax seals and other stamps, and some writing in black Indian ink.

This read: *To the Water Rat, Rat's House, The River Bank, the River, nr The Town, Capital of the Empire.*

"Well!" said Ratty. "This doesn't tell us much, now does it!"

But then he saw that some extra words of guidance had been added less legibly after the address: *The River lies sou'-sou'-west of the Town, and maybe three days' good walking, a day by boat.*

The Rat repeated this slowly, then muttered, "Well, it's from a mariner of some kind, that's plain enough, but who?"

He turned suddenly to the Mole and was about to say something when the young rat, silent still, pointed to the twine once more, about part of which was wrapped some of that oiled paper used by seafarers to keep their shag in good order.

The Water Rat opened it up and then, seeking to find

the best light he could, he read aloud the strangest, and the most moving letter he was ever likely to receive.

"Dear Mr Water Rat,

"I hope I may make so bold as to trust you remember me after all these long years and that time we spent upon the roadside near your home, when you made me as sailor-like a repast as ever I've had before or since. I am that same —

"Why, Mole," cried Ratty, his suspicions now confirmed, "it's from the Sea Rat. The one I met so many years ago. *You* remember!"

The Mole did indeed remember, only too well. It was a story he had told Nephew a good many times as a warning against yielding too impulsively to those restless yearnings for travel that beset so many animals of a wandering nature at autumn time. He had told him of how that stranger had appeared along the River Bank, and held the Rat spellbound with many alluring tales of far distant places; of how the Mole had come along just in time to restrain the Rat from following in the stranger's footsteps and leaving the River Bank for ever, to end up one day in a watery grave at the bottom of some foreign dock (as the Mole imagined such wandering seafarers too often ended their days).

The Rat resumed his reading of the letter:

"I am that same Sea Rat to whom you were so hospitable, and I have never forgotten your kindness or the River Bank where you had your home.

"Well, fellow mariner, the game's up with me now and I have

*not many days to live, mayhap only hours. By the time you read
this, shipmate, I'll be down below in Davy Jones's locker."*

For the first time since they had entered the cage the
young rat responded in some way: he nodded sadly. It
was evident that the Sea Rat had indeed passed on, just
as he had predicted.

*"Now, here's the point. I remember you to be a practical
kind of fellow, as most nautical rats are, so I'll not beat about
the bush. After I left you those many years ago, fate and good
fortune took me to the creeks of Malaya where I gave up the
sea-faring life for a time and made a stab at rubber plantation
work. But I lost what money I had, and I lost as well the
only pearl I ever possessed in all my life – the mother of that
youngster you see before you now."*

"The poor youth!" cried the Mole, much moved by
the Sea Rat's testimony.

*"I decided to work my passage home but was diverted up the
Nile, where they have need of a good hand upon a deck, which
I was, and which my boy had by then become. But lady luck
went against me once more, and not a fortnight since I contracted
a fever, what we would call the 'Gruesome' in our lingo.
"I said before that the boy's mother was the brightest pearl
in my life, but not far behind is the boy himself. He's good
about the water, so you'll have a use for him and he'll work
his passage without you needing to train him up. He can
speak five languages fluently, and two more passably, though
you may not have much use for Malayan lingo and its dialects*

along the River Bank, nor Chinese for all I know.

"I've racked my brain as to what to do with him, for this place is filled with villains and low types, so once I'm gone he'll be lucky not to be sold into slavery and bondage. Anyway, the sea's no life for a rat these days, for now the sailing ships have all but gone there's no joy left in it. Come to that, the roaming life's not all it's cracked up to be. That was why I had been trying to get him back home and apprentice him to landlubbing work of some kind; but I'll not be able to now.

"All in all, and when I count the little money I have left, which isn't much, the best thing I can do for him, which will let me die in the hope he's got a bit of a start in life, is to send him to you. Seeing as I don't have enough to buy a ticket for him as a passenger, except to get him as far as Sicily, where I don't put his chances too high, I thought I'd send him by the Colonial Royal Mail, which will give him feed and water, and get him home safer than if he was the Crown Jewels, which to me he is.

"So that's the long and short of it. There should be a bit of change left over, which you're welcome to, and I know he'll more than make up for the trouble he's causing you. Don't mind if he don't say much till he's near water. He don't like to be away from it too long. Farewell, old shipmate, and look after my lad for me proper, and teach him all you know. And don't let him wander off till he's learnt how to settle down, as you have but I never did.

"Regulations won't allow livestock to have baggage, but then seafarers like me travel light. Still, I've hung me old marlin spike about his neck so he'll have something to remember me by. I've had it since my first ship and now it'll have to travel on without me.

"Your old friend,

"Sea Rat."

Ratty stood in silence for a moment, and then signalled to Mole to come with him out of the cage.

"Whatever am I going to do, Mole? I can't possibly take him home with me. Yet I can't very well leave him here, can I? Why, this young rat is absolutely nothing to do with me, and it is very presumptuous of that old sea dog –"

"You haven't forgotten him, then?"

"Of course not. I have often thought of him, but now –"

"But now he's gone, Ratty, as we all will one day, and he's left you the only thing he had to leave."

"Well, I suppose you could put it that way."

"And he has entrusted that 'item' to the only animal in all the world – and I daresay he met a great many in his time – upon whom he felt he could rely."

"Well . . . " began the Rat, weakening. But then he looked down the aisle to that unkempt, dirtily dressed stranger, and he thought of his own small quarters, ship-shape and orderly. No, he couldn't possibly . . .

"I won't do it, Mole!" cried Ratty. "Why, if I let go of the tiller now upon the stormy and uncertain waters of the Sea Rat's presumption, and your wrong-headed persuasion, there's no knowing where I'll run aground!"

"And what did you advise when Nephew turned up at my door, Ratty?" said the Mole, who in circumstances such as these could be formidable. "Did you tell me to send him packing?"

"No, I suppose I didn't."

"Did you not tell me to put up with it? Did you not suggest that it might even do me some good?"

"I suppose I might have said some such thing," conceded the Rat grudgingly.

"And that it might make me a little less self-centred?"

"Yes, yes, Mole, I did think those things, and I do think them. But Nephew is one thing, and a relative to boot; but this young fellow . . . why no, I won't do it and that's final!"

With a fierce and irritable look on his face, Ratty turned back to the cage to give his decision.

The youngster looked very frightened and sorry for himself. He certainly was grubby, and hungry, too.

"Well, sir," said the Post Office official, joining them once more. "Having seen the item, are you to accept it or send it back? Naturally, it makes no difference to us, as under recent agreements with the government of Egypt return passage is paid for in the case of non-acceptance, and in the circumstances I would quite understand."

"Humph," said the Rat, glowering.

"If *you* won't, Ratty," cried the Mole, much distressed, "let *me* take him in, for though my home is small, I can surely find space!"

"Ah!" said the Post Office official. "Now that would not be permitted, no, not at all. It must be the addressee who accepts, or nobody, and as I say, returns of such items are quite a regular occurrence. Those parrots you saw will be on their way back next week, seeing as they don't speak English. If you do not wish to accept the item, then it would simply be a matter of completing the correct paperwork, and then shipping the item to Egypt again. That item could be back in Cairo in less than a year."

"Hmmm," growled the Rat, frowning even more.

"But, Ratty," interrupted Nephew, "you cannot possibly send him back! At least you could see if he knows something about river-work by asking him some questions. He might be useful to you."

The Water Rat went closer to the item in question, and after some thought asked, "You can scull a boat, I suppose?"

The item nodded.

"Tie a bowline?"

The item nodded.

"Tack and gybe and punt one-handed across a five-knot current in a Force Six wind?"

The item nodded a third time.

"What can't you do?" said the Rat grumpily.

The item frowned thoughtfully and finally spoke.

"Can't swim," it said.

"Can't swim!" cried the Rat. "Did you hear that, Mole. Here is a rat, brought up on the water, and he can't swim! Can't swim, indeed. Well, I'm not having a water rat going out into the world who can't swim: it's not right, it's not dignified and it's not good for my kind's reputation. Imagine how eagles would feel if one of their number went about in public who couldn't fly!"

"He'd have to walk," said Nephew, winking at the "item" to indicate that despite Ratty's huffing and puffing he was on the way to coming round a little. Though a wink must have seemed a poor weight to set upon the balance of that animal's future expectation against the frowns, glowering, and determined words the Rat had so far spoken, and so he continued to look very frightened and pathetic.

"Or imagine," continued the Rat, "a rabbit that couldn't burrow or —"

"Yes, yes, Ratty," said the Mole, intervening. "So what are you going to do about it?"

"He can stay with me till he's learnt to swim."

"And then he can stay a little longer," said Nephew, feeling perhaps that this was the moment to set the future straight for the young rat, "till he has, as his father put it so fairly, 'worked his passage'."

"So you'll accept the item, sir?" enquired the Post Office official.

The Rat nodded curtly, and signed the card offered him.

He did not linger once his decision was made, but on the way back to their craft he sought to insist that they visit a clothes shop to kit out the newcomer in something clean and decent. But once more the sensitive Mole intervened, saying that since his clothes were the only possessions the youngster had from his past life, apart from the marlin spike about his neck, perhaps he might feel more comfortable hanging on to them a short while longer, grubby and heathen though they were.

"I am sure that Nephew here, who is about his size, or Master Toad, who has a very extensive wardrobe, will be happy to kit him out for a time till he can make his own choice."

"Humph!" said the Rat, who had not yet so much as smiled upon the poor youngster, or given him the slightest encouragement.

But then, as they reached the end of a narrow street and turned the last corner, the River, with all the jetties and boats and multifarious activity of a busy riverfront, came into view, and a heart-warming change immediately came over the young rat.

Till that moment he had stayed close by the Mole, for he was frightened and confused and the Mole seemed the only friendly thing about. The horses, the carts, the shouting of street-sellers and the honking of occasional motor-cars had been almost too much for him.

Now there was the River, and in the air its watery scent. The youngster stopped quite suddenly. Thinking that there was difficulty or danger about, the Mole stopped as well, while a little way off, where he had been walking along huffily, the Rat also came to a halt, slowed by the sight of the River perhaps, but caught still more by the expression on the youth's face.

The fear had gone from his eyes, the confusion, too, and had all the horses and carts and people in the world descended upon that very spot, it would not have mattered one whit. A dreamy, vacant look had come to his face, and even as the Mole started to urge him on, for they could not stand in everyone's way at so busy a junction, it was the Rat's turn to be sensitive.

He raised a hand to still his good friend the Mole, and they watched together as the youngster, like a pigeon flying home to roost, made his own way towards the River's edge. Slowly and dreamily he went, not quite looking here, nor quite there, yet taking in everything at once by sight and sense, and by touch as well. His hands felt the worn metal-hooped bollards as he passed them as if they were old friends, lingered on a barge half hauled out of the water, and finally found a resting place on a rope that ran down from the barge in a great sweeping curve to the water, where it was tied fast to an upright timber.

On this rope the youngster leaned his weight, and then gently rocked back and forth, as if to shed from himself all the cares he had carried so long alone. Those watching him could not but reflect how hard his journey must have been, how alarming, and how often he must have wondered what his final destination would be.

Having lingered thus at peace for a time, watching the River's flow and all its varied currents near and far, he let go of the rope and went to sit upon a wooden jetty, his feet dangling over its high edge down towards the water.

He sat quite still there, as if considering something, till at last he cocked his head to one side, listening, then raised one hand and finally another, and moved them gently to and fro.

"But he's . . . " began Nephew, for he had only ever seen one other animal do what the youngster was doing now.

"He *is!*" whispered the Mole with delight.

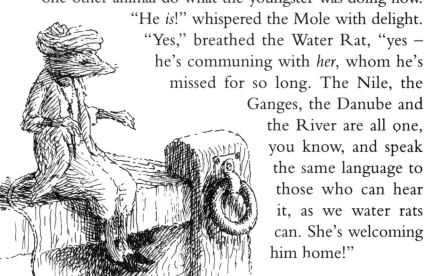

"Yes," breathed the Water Rat, "yes — he's communing with *her*, whom he's missed for so long. The Nile, the Ganges, the Danube and the River are all one, you know, and speak the same language to those who can hear it, as we water rats can. She's welcoming him home!"

Ratty stepped over and joined him, and they sat together for a while, till he was finally ready – long after the Mole thought they should have left if they were ever to get back to Toad Hall in time for dinner – and they all headed over to where Toad's craft was moored.

Of the youngster's pleasure at going aboard, of his insistence on examining its every nook and cranny and working part, of the dangerous way he had of expertly skipping about from bow to stern, from one side of the deck to another, why, any boatman would understand and need no description.

That he was an expert upon deck there was no doubt, for he cast off the painter with a skill excelled only by the Rat's own, and set the rope ready and right for landing later just as the Rat himself liked to do. Nor was there a moment upon that voyage back to Toad's estate when his eyes were not upon the boat or the River, or rather both at once, just as the Rat's always were.

As they came within sight of Toad's estate at last, Ratty said, "You can take the helm."

This was a high honour from Ratty, and the youngster jumped to as quick as a flash, while the Mole, who had always had trouble steering Toad's great craft, sat back and admired the way he handled her, smooth and safe.

"Watch the cross wind as we round the final bend," sang out Ratty happily.

But the youth had already seen the tell-tale signs of the breeze in the trees along the bank ahead and had turned the prow a shade windward moments before.

"Will you take her in?" called out the Rat, when Toad's boat-house came into view.

"Aye aye, sir!" sang out the youth, as merrily as any sub-lieutenant in the Royal Navy to his captain.

"We'll moor her first and set our passengers to land and put her into the boat-house later. Now cut the —"

But the Rat had no need to complete his instruction, even though the evening wind was stronger across the bows than he normally liked, for the engine was cut just as the Rat would have done it, and the youngster grasped an oar and, using it as a rudder and not punting it as the Rat might have done, he settled the craft in its berth as sweetly as a broad-bean in its pod.

Otter and Portly, who were sitting on the jetty, their eyes wide in astonishment, could not believe what they saw: the Rat standing on the prow, painter in hand, while a grubby-looking fellow wearing clothes out of Arabia, like a boatman from a Bible tale, was at the helm of Toad's great craft, and apparently knew what he was about.

"What's that?" said the Otter, as Ratty jumped ashore and made the painter fast.

"Livestock," said Ratty with a smile.

"Livestock?" repeated Portly, catching and making fast the other painter that the helmsman threw.

"He'll be working his passage with me for a time," added Ratty, by way of further explanation.

Mole and Nephew were helped off the craft, like passengers from an ocean-going liner, while the Water Rat's apprentice leaned his weight against the oar in the water to keep the craft steady as a rock.

"Doesn't seem to need much further education before you grant him his articles," said the Otter dryly, and with considerable respect.

71

"He can't swim, though," said the Rat, "and that takes a lot of learning if you come to it late in life."

"I suppose it does," said the Otter with a grin.

The young rat was last ashore and he wobbled about for the first few steps as sailormen often do. Then he stared up at Toad Hall, where the lights were just coming on for the evening, and he said, "Is that your home, Mr Water Rat, sir?"

For the first time that day Ratty laughed out loud.

"No, no – that's the famous Mr Toad's house, where we're having supper tonight. *My* home's further along the River Bank, where a water rat's should be. We'll not make passage down there till midnight or later if I know Toad, but if you get tired, don't worry, Toad'll find a berth for you tonight."

At that moment they spotted Toad up on his terrace, Master Toad at his side, both waving a greeting, for if there was one thing the two agreed on full-heartedly, it was the importance of welcoming guests.

So up through Toad's garden they all went, happy and hungry after a good day's work, livestock and all.

· IV ·
The Beast of the Iron Bridge

The strange and tragic circumstances of the arrival of the Sea Rat's son, and Ratty's decision to accept him as a live-in assistant (Able Seaman, First Class), naturally attracted a good deal of attention and gossip along the River Bank.

It is in the nature of society, however, even one so generally benign and peaceable as that of which Badger, Rat, Mole and Mr Toad of Toad Hall were the leaders, to grow bored with talking about things when they go right, and to look about instead for things that are going wrong. The River Bank did not have far to look or long to wait before it found a subject of general debate and concern – and alarm as well.

It was but a few days after the Rat's return from the Town, when a chill September dusk was settling upon the River and the moorhens were clucking their good-nights, just as the first stars began to show, that an extra-ordinary and terrifying creature made an appearance near the Iron Bridge.

Two of Mr Toad's employees, an apprentice gardener and a scullery maid, who were then walking out together, were lingering in the gloaming upon the Iron Bridge and ignoring the cold, as such sweethearts will, when they were alarmed to see a loathsome and malev-olent creature approaching them from the direction of the Wild Wood.

In their determination to get as far away from the terrible apparition as possible, they fled blindly in the opposite direction, past the entrance to Toad Hall and some time later found themselves at Mole End, in a frightened and dishevelled state.

"Lor', sir," the maid told the Mole when he had taken them in and offered them a comforting drink, "he was as big as a tree, and rasped and groaned in anger as he came towards us!"

"Did you not catch a glimpse of the stranger's face?" asked the Mole.

"I tell you, sir, that were no human thing we saw!" cried the swain. "He had great eyes that shone all white and carried a stave as high as a church steeple, I swear it!"

Since the couple were unwilling to return to Toad Hall alone, Mole and Nephew put on their boots and overcoats, and Mole took up his trusty cudgel, the same one the Rat had given him many years before. Thus armed, though dubious of the foolish couple's claims, they accompanied them to Toad Hall by way of the bridge, where they even ventured to shine a storm lantern in the general direction of the Wild Wood to satisfy themselves there were no real monsters about.

They found nothing, and having returned the maid and her lover safely to the arms, respectively, of the Housekeeper and the Head Gardener at Toad Hall, proceeded to Toad's drawing room, where they discussed the matter over some excellent mulled wine.

Their news threw their host into a state of panic that seemed excessive even by Toad's standards. After ordering every window and door to be securely bolted, he summoned the Head Gardener to see if there might be some explanation of the event.

"Aye, sir, I have talked to the lad and know him to be a sober and sensible fellow. If you ask me, this is a return of that foul fiend who terrorized the River Bank in my great-grandfather's day."

"And what fiend was that?" asked Toad nervously.

"The Beast of the Iron Bridge," said the Head Gardener darkly, his brow furrowing. "Aye, so evil and dangerous was he, that the women and children, my grandparents among 'em, were evercated to the Town, and the men lay in wait at night to catch 'im, and put a wooden stake through his heart."

"Do you hear that, Mole?" cried Toad, jumping up and mopping his brow. "The Beast is back and we're in mortal danger and must arm ourselves with guns and cannons!"

But the Mole was laughing.

"If I remember correctly, for I investigated the story some years ago in my pursuit of local history, the so-called 'Beast' proved to be no more than a drunken vagrant from Lathbury way sleeping rough by the bridge for a week or two."

"If you say so, sir," said the Head Gardener darkly, "if you do say so. But us more unediccated folk, who have reason to go by way of the Iron Bridge and on into the Wild Wood once in a while, and have discussed the matter with the weasels and stoats, have heard and seen things, monstrous and terrible things. That there Beast do come up out of the undergrowth every hundred years and eat up babbies and older folk!"

"Older folk?" gasped Toad, whose eyes were almost popping out of his head in terror.

"*And* younger folk, for 'e likes young flesh, they do say, if 'e can get 'is claws into it."

"Claws?" sobbed Master Toad who, for all his youthful hauteur and blustering, was no less a craven coward than his guardian.

"Now then," said the Mole, taking command of the situation and bringing the Head Gardener's lurid talk to an abrupt end, "that will be all, that's quite enough!"

"We are besieged! We are in mortal danger!" wailed Toad and his ward, clutching each other in an unexpected display of unity in their mutual hour of need.

76

It was only after they had supped a good deal more mulled wine, and the Mole had thoughtfully retired to the kitchen to create one of his soothing Nutmeg and Sloe sedatives and agreed to sleep outside Toad's bedroom door, cudgel at the ready, that his friends calmed down.

By morning Toad had his fears under control once more, and after three more days, when there was no sign of the Beast, despite a careful nocturnal watch by a good many of the more sturdy River Bank folk, Mr Toad was back to his normal cheerful self.

So it was a very great pity that on the fourth evening

after the first sighting it was Master Toad of all animals who had the next encounter with the Beast, in the company of Otter, Portly and Young Rat (as the River Bank folk had decided to call him). They had been out doing River work, and were just disembarking from Ratty's boat and another the Otter sometimes used, both full of the dead reeds and foliage they had cut down, when . . . there it was!

"Mon Dieu!" cried Master Toad, reverting to his native tongue in his panic and fear. "There! *Ah non!* O!"

He pointed a trembling finger at the bridge as the others scrambled onto the bank. Even the normally fearless Otter was struck dumb by what he saw.

A huge, strange, hunchbacked figure on the bridge, ghastly eyes white and shining just as the two lovers had claimed, and carrying an enormous thick stave that might easily strike all of them down with one blow.

It seemed to see them and moved to descend the bridge towards them. Only the Otter's stolid stance and Young Rat's calm kept Master Toad and Portly from fleeing headlong in the opposite direction.

"Here you, what do you want?" cried the Otter boldly, while Young Rat sensibly took up a boathook and held it out most threateningly.

This seemed enough to halt the Beast's advance, for it paused and stared at them awhile, its huge head swaying from side to side, before it turned away, went back over the bridge and disappeared over the far side, where it was lost in the mists and shadows of the evening.

"Did you hear its rasping, groaning voice?" said Master Toad.

"Did you see its thick, clawed hands?" cried Portly.

Considerably chastened, the four animals retreated along the bank to the Rat's house. That brave and resourceful animal listened with some scepticism at first, for like the Mole he was no believer in ghosts and beasts, but knowing the Otter to be an utterly reliable witness, and impressed by Young Rat's calm affirmation of what his old friend reported, he was finally inclined to take the matter seriously. But as for it being the legendary Beast of the Wild Wood . . .

"Beast, indeed!" declared the Rat dismissively. "It is probably some wanderer who is the worse for drink. He has no business frightening folk like that – what he needs is a good drubbing, and that's what he'll receive if I get my hands on him!"

"That's just what my uncle has been saying," observed Nephew.

"Well, if you'd come with us today you could have given him that drubbing there and then," said the Otter, who had been surprised when the Rat had declined to join them for River work that day.

"I had business in the kitchen," explained the Rat. "Nephew reminded me that it is Mole's birthday tomorrow and though that modest and retiring animal has never celebrated the event with a party before we felt that he should do so now. Nephew has arranged for Mole to call on me at lunchtime tomorrow, leaving him a clear run to prepare Mole End for our surprise, and make some sandwiches and so forth. I shall ferry Mole back, and bring with me the cake I have spent the day baking."

The Rat led them to his stove and showed them the currant cake he had made, which was covered in white icing upon which he had inscribed the message "For Our Friend Mole, Happy Birthday!" along with a picture of the Mole sitting in the Rat's boat, in which the two friends had spent so many happy hours.

"Why, Ratty, I am most impressed," said the Otter warmly.

"And so will Mole be, I hope," said the Rat, "when we all meet on his doorstep tomorrow at three in the afternoon and surprise him with a party! I have asked Badger to make sure that Toad arrives on time — we all know his irritating propensity for lateness. Master Toad, there is no need to look so smug, for you are not much better in my experience! Now where were we?"

By the time they had finished their ruminations on the subject of the Beast the hour was late. As the Rat's home was too small for them all, the Otter took Master Toad back to his own home, where it was proposed that he should stay the night, whilst Nephew was quickly ferried back across the River to take the short route up to Mole End.

The Otter was very much surprised to hear Master Toad say as he reached his house, "You know, Otter old chap, it's good of you to offer me a bed, but I ought to be getting back."

"Toad won't miss you overnight," said the Otter heartily. "He knows you're in good hands."

"Well, that's just it, you see, he's imposed a curfew on me till I return to school. I should have been back in the study at six for a final hour of work and in bed by half past seven with the light out. It's most irksome but he's threatened not to pay my school fees! I should have been back long ago really."

The Otter laughed to see how Toad had imposed his will on the wayward youth, and was about to offer to accompany him home when to their surprise Toad himself suddenly appeared out of the darkness, lantern in hand.

"Is that you, Otter? I was looking for . . . ah, there he is, skulking about and —"

"Not at all, Monsieur Toad, you see we —"

But the Otter put a hand on Master Toad's arm to quieten him. They had already agreed not to mention the second sighting of the Beast to Toad lest it upset him, and caused him to do something foolish such as hire a posse of armed guards.

"My fault, Toad," interposed the Otter. "Late getting back from our River work, at which Master Toad has excelled himself by the way. He was just saying he must hurry home and was willing to do so alone, despite that scare we had some nights ago."

"Pooh to that!" said Toad. "That was just some stuff and nonsense that gardeners and scullery maids dream up. Nothing that honest and upright citizens such as ourselves need fear or even give a second thought to."

"So you're not nervous of the Beast, Toad?" said the Otter, who had been very surprised indeed to see him walking about alone at night.

"Me? Not a bit!" cried Toad. "Now, come on, Master Toad; it's late and you need sleep, for tomorrow —"

"Yes, Pater? What shall we do tomorrow?"

A grim and determined look came upon Toad's face.

"Tomorrow you shall begin that educational exercise I promised you."

"*Ah, non!*" groaned the youth.

"O *yes!*" declared Toad.

With that, and a wave of farewell to the Otter, the determined Toad led his ward back over the bridge.

"But are you not frightened at all, Monsieur Toad?"

said the youth with very considerable respect as they approached Toad Hall.

"Not at all," said Toad, feeling the revolver, three knives and sabre he had secreted beneath his coat, just in case. "No, not at all."

On the whole, Toad was thus far well pleased with his campaign to bring Master Toad to heel, and instruct him in the pleasures of healthy routine, self-discipline and the academic arts and sciences. His threat to remove his ward from school and send him off to earn his own living seemed to have had a most salutary and beneficial effect. The youth had gone to bed early every night, woken each morning in good time for breakfast, and then risen from the table of his own accord and headed off to the study, where he worked diligently on all the exercises and items of reading set for him.

Why, he had even attempted to engage Toad in conversation about aspects of topography, geometry, trigonometry and the history of the colonies and the French Revolution! Toad's knowledge of such things was a little rusty, to say the least, but that did not prevent him from giving his views on all five subjects, as well as certain aspects of Shakespearean tragedy and comedy that he thought Master Toad might find helpful.

Toad's only regret was the gloomy feeling that came over him when he himself had to practise the austere habits he now daily preached over the breakfast table. His plight was somewhat eased, however, by certain private arrangements he had made with his butler. It was not so hard sticking to the healthful regime of orange juice, thin un-buttered toast, a solitary egg (poached) and single slice of bacon (lean) once a week that he had prescribed for them both, when he knew that a full English breakfast plus buttered crumpets (so necessary to stave off the advance of winter) were awaiting him in his bedroom, once he had packed his ward off to the study each morning at a quarter to nine.

"Aaah . . . !" sighed Toad, who was rediscovering certain lost pleasures of youth as he tucked into his secret second daily breakfast, such as the fact that scrumped apples taste a good deal better than those honestly obtained.

It was true he was a mite puzzled that Master Toad seemed to be taking his medicine so willingly and without complaint, but then he remembered that he himself had taught the youngster the arts of cunning and deception. No doubt the youth had established his own lines of supply for extra sustenance, and no doubt they involved the Housekeeper (whom Master Toad had long since charmed) and certain drawers and shelves in the library as hiding places which Toad might himself have used.

One day soon, Master Toad would be off into the world and there he would discover that very often the end justified the means, and Toad felt sure he would be grateful for the lessons directly and indirectly taught him that autumn.

Toad ruminated on these matters as he led his ward back to Toad Hall that night. But as they went inside and Master Toad compliantly headed off to bed with only one final plea – "Pater, are we really to go 'iking tomorrow?" – which Toad ignored, he turned his thoughts to the one area in which he had so far failed.

For the youth had successfully avoided each and every one of the planned afternoon sessions of educational exercise by resorting to all the tricks in the book, and many more that Toad had never come across.

Master Toad had been afflicted by sprained ankles, headaches, upset stomachs, grumbling appendices, double vision, fainting fits and many other physical ailments, as well as some mental ones, all of the kind that can be relied on to disappear the moment darkness descends and the threat of educational exercise has receded for another day, and dinner is in the offing.

So successful had these stratagems been, and so easily had Toad been daily defeated on this front, that his ward had begun to suspect that his pater's heart was no more taken by the idea of hiking than his own. Indeed, he had the smug sense that the battle was won, and there would be no more talk of hiking from Mr Toad.

In this he was nearly right, but finally wrong. For Toad had indeed found the notion of hiking considerably to his distaste, and the vast stock of hiking equipment he had ordered up from a well-known emporium in the Town used to dealing with military needs had at first baffled and alarmed him. Its sheer weight was dispiriting for a start, for Toad had quickly realized that what was not to be worn was to be carried. Then, too, there was the difficulty of working out what each item of equipment was meant to do. Hobnail boots were easy enough, as were water bottles. But dangerous-looking knives? A mosquito net? And a spade that looked like a pick? For what strange reason were these supplied to a gentleman who wished to take a healthful stroll in the countryside?

Eventually, on Badger's wise advice, he ordered several books on the subject of hiking, which was then attracting a good deal of attention from authors good and bad, experienced and inexperienced. Toad was no great reader and had eyed them askance for several days after their arrival. But then one morning, after a second helping of scrambled eggs and black pudding in his bedroom, Toad dipped into one of the tomes, and was fascinated by what he found there.

Stories of hikes through the Pyrenees (child's play), accounts of the ascent of Mont Blanc (easy) and climbs in the Zillertaler in Austria (more problematic), and a race against a killer blizzard up the north face of the Eiger (nigh impossible).

All this, and a great deal more, Toad found he could achieve over an extended breakfast while seated in the comfort of a padded chair by his bedroom window, gazing out from time to time at the advance of autumn across the River Bank.

"Yes, yes!" he would sigh, resting his book on his plump and contented stomach, and imagining himself leading an expedition to . . .

"Everest! I shall be its conqueror!"

"Sir?" his butler would interrupt him. "Would you care for some fresh coffee before partaking of your mid-morning bath?"

"Yes, yes!" cried the ecstatic Toad, returning to his book.

Though thus now persuaded that in theory at least hiking had a lot to commend it, Toad might very easily have got no further in his examination of the expensive equipment so impulsively bought and now safely stowed in the gun room, had his eye not alighted one day upon a book somewhat slimmer than the others, and of more austere aspect.

"Hmmm, what's this then?" Toad said to himself. "I don't seem to have seen it before."

Even as he read the title and the author's name, he felt a thrill of vocation and purpose, and knew at once this was the light in the hiking darkness he had been seeking.

"Yes, O yes!" he whispered as he turned the pages, reading every word and each terse chapter with mounting speed and excitement, for here at last was a book that told him in terms he could understand how to deal – *exactly* how to deal – with those who refused to follow a leader's command in matters of educational exercise: in short, those like Master Toad.

The book was entitled *Hiking For Leaders With Novices: Do's, Don't's and Definitely Not's*, by Colonel J. R. Wheeler Senior, Member of the Alpine Club and Hiking Adviser to the Royal Marines School of Music (Yachting Section).

It was that felicitous phrase "Leaders With Novices" that so appealed to Toad, for a leader he felt himself to be, and with a novice he would be venturing forth.

Wheeler, an ex-Indian Army officer and conqueror of the Nangha-Dhal in the Himalaya, had a good deal to say on all aspects of hiking, and was especially strong on boots, maps, thornproof breeches and hunting knives. He had a good section on protective headgear (against falling rocks) and goggles (against sand and snow), which he felt should be worn at all times, and an invaluable few pages on certain technicalities often overlooked in lesser tomes upon the subject, namely rope work, compass work and night-craft. But it was in his excellent writing on the art of effective leadership, about which Toad already felt himself to know a good deal, that Wheeler won his latest reader's heart and mind.

Wheeler's notion of leadership was clear and to the point:

> *The leader is <u>leader</u>, and must at all times be on his guard against insubordination and the dangers of paying too much attention to the weak and feeble in his group. These must be weeded out and made an example of.*
>
> *Where native porters are concerned, the leader is advised always to hire two or three extra (on my Nangha-Dhal Expedition I took on an extra porter for every four days of the journey, but conditions were extreme) so that they might be disposed of en route to encourage the others not to slacken.*
>
> *The good leader will always remain in front and not allow another to take his place there, otherwise, like the African pack lion, he is done for . . .*

Wheeler's advice on a range of matters was of a kind that appealed especially to one such as Toad:

> *It will frequently happen, and a leader should certainly not be disheartened by this, that the way will be lost. I make it a practice, and I urge novice leaders to learn from my mistakes and follow this advice rigorously, on no account to tell others in my party where I intend going. This ensures that wherever one may arrive, one appears to have intended that as one's destination.*

But it was another piece of advice in the book that finally gave Toad the will to try out the equipment he had avoided actually using for so many weeks.

> *The true leader should not feel obliged to know or understand the use of every piece of equipment or the practice of every technique, for he will have employed those in his expedition who should be able and willing advisers on such matters. However, the effective leader will need to appreciate the importance of <u>seeming</u> to know what he is talking about and <u>looking</u> as if he knows what he is doing. This inspires confidence in those he leads, and keeps them at their tasks.*
>
> *Therefore, a leader is strongly advised to try on the equipment till he is used to wearing it, and to find some quiet place where, unobserved, he can get the 'feel' of it with a short solo hike or two. In this way he will ensure that he looks the part.*

Thus instructed, Toad had risen from his reading couch and that very evening, having ensured Master Toad was at his academic labours, repaired to the gun room to begin his further familiarization with hiking equipment.

With Colonel Wheeler's help he was pleased to discover the purpose of the prismatic compass, but since it was difficult to hold and read, clearly faulty (the needle seemed to wobble about a good deal and refused to stay in the same place) *and* heavy, he discarded it.

Wheeler's book made rather more sense for Toad of an item for which he had been unable to see a use, but which once explained he saw as an essential. This was an alpenstock, a thick, rude stave almost as tall as himself, with a heavy iron spike at one end, deadly sharp.

> *Apart from being an emblem of leadership, the alpenstock is useful for a great many purposes, such as killing game, the light disciplining of porters, bridging crevasses, forming stretchers and, in extremis, quelling native rebellions.*

Toad trusted that its primary usage, as symbol and prop to his leadership, was the only one on this impressive list he would need it for, and took up the huge stick with relish, holding it aloft like a crusader's sword and inadvertently striking the ceiling above.

Now feeling, as so often in his life, that nothing ventured was nothing gained, Toad quickly donned the thornproof suit and cap, hoisted the large haversack up onto his shoulders, placed the goggles over his eyes against sandstorms and, holding his trusty alpenstock, opened the gun-room door to check that there was nobody about.

Seeing the coast was clear, he made his way through

the conservatory and out into the dusk, and headed down towards the River Bank. When he reached the Iron Bridge, he struggled up its steep face in a slow and measured way (it reminded him of his imaginary ascent some evenings before of Mont Blanc) and found himself trotting down the other side in an alarmingly accelerating manner (the weight of the haversack, albeit stuffed only with wrapping paper, was not quite what he was used to) and straight into the hedge beside the road.

There he rested awhile till, imagining he heard voices and feeling suddenly nervous to be out in the dark alone, he gripped his trusty alpenstock, leant on it as he pulled himself up and turned back towards his home. The goggles did not greatly improve his vision, and fancying he saw the outline of people upon the bridge he raised them up to rest upon his forehead. Then, seeing that he was mistaken, he continued his journey home unobserved, stowed away the gear and joined the unsuspecting Master Toad for supper.

It was after dinner that night – over a glass of mulled wine – that Mole and Nephew brought the news of the sighting that sent Toad into such a panic. To think that even as he had been climbing the Iron Bridge, a malevolent creature was skulking somewhere nearby! He rapidly dropped his plans to put his hiking equipment through another test the following night, and decided to restrict his research to the safety of his own bedroom.

As the days went by with no further sightings, however, his initial panic gradually lessened. He began to agree with Mole's view that the "Beast" was merely some vagrant, who was not likely to be seen again.

Having thus reassured himself and dipped once more into Colonel Wheeler's excellent book, he decided to take advantage of his ward's absence to try again.

This time he put a few light items in his haversack to test his mettle, and once more headed off for the Iron Bridge in his alpine outfit, feeling it would be wise to ascend and descend a few times as training for his back and calf muscles.

He saw no sign of the Beast, but after a while he heard boat-like sounds from the River and guessed that Otter, Master Toad and the others were coming back after their day of River work. So confident by now did he feel of his attire, and so monarch-like did he feel with the alpenstock in his hand, that at first he thought he might go and greet them and reveal his new pursuit.

But he thought again, for the gloaming would not show his gear in its fullest splendour, and he felt suddenly very tired. As he strove to climb the humped bridge once more, his breath came out in grunts and groans, and the haversack seemed to weigh him down even more. So he turned about, went home and enjoyed an invigorating supper before venturing out to find Master Toad, and make clear his resolve to brook no further excuses and to take him hiking the very next day.

As they returned home together, Toad was pleased and gratified that Master Toad seemed so obedient, and stuck so close by his side. Indeed he seemed very eager to get home to bed and so be ready for the morrow.

"Monsieur," he declared, using that form of address he reserved for formal occasions when a certain respect for his elders was called for, "I 'ave an admission to

94

make. Tonight we 'ave seen the Beast – an hour or two before you came."

"The Beast of the Iron Bridge?" gasped Toad.

"On that bridge 'e stood, threatening us! Yet as we walked back later you, my guardian, showed no fear!"

Toad suddenly felt rather faint. "I – I did not know –" he spluttered.

"You were brave and bold and gave me much confidence. Tomorrow, Pater, I will follow your lead in 'iking wherever you wish, and I shall not complain!"

With these grand and respectful words Master Toad retired to bed, leaving Toad astonished and bewildered as he stared out of the conservatory window to see if he might espy the Beast, but saw only his own reflection.

·V·
Mole's Birthday Surprise

Mole and Ratty were sitting on Ratty's porch with mugs of tea in their hands and shawls over their knees. Having enjoyed a lingering lunch by the fireside, they were now making the most of the Indian summer by watching the River drift by in this companionable way.

"Do you know, Mole," observed the Rat, "I cannot now remember a time when we did not know each other, and were constantly able to look forward – and back! – to picnic and tea, courtesy yourself, and blissful days afloat, courtesy my boat."

"And your skill," said the Mole.

"That's as maybe," said the Rat, "but the fact is that one way and another we have a good deal to be thankful for, have we not?"

It was not often that the Rat mused thus, and the Mole was rather surprised at it, but then he knew very well that the Rat had not been quite himself lately. He had seemed more often tired than in yesteryear, and a little more inclined to stay in his seat enjoying an extra cup of tea or two than to embark on some urgent River errand.

The Mole did not in the least object to lingering in the Rat's company in this way, for there was no friendship that gave him more constant and lasting pleasure. These days the opportunities to do so at the Rat's house were rarer, for Young Rat was in residence, and daily giving the Rat much assistance and quiet company. But that day he had gone off with the Otter and Portly, and Mole told himself, wrongly as it happened, that was why the Rat had invited him over.

In fact, it was Mole's birthday and Ratty was mischievously enjoying the fact that his friend thought he had forgotten the date altogether. Indeed, he had been careful to make no reference to the Mole's birthday, and had given no hint of the surprise in store, though he had second thoughts when he saw a brief look of disappointment in the Mole's eyes when he first saw their little repast and realized there was no obvious sign of extra festivity.

"His surprise and pleasure will be all the greater," the Rat told himself, hoping that Nephew had risen to the task and even now was preparing Mole End for the surprise celebratory tea. To maintain the secret, he had been careful to stow away in his boat the special cake he had made.

He proposed to ferry the Mole back across the River at half past two, at about the time he expected others to begin making their way to Mole End.

Yet any initial disappointment the Mole might have felt had soon evaporated before that mutual feeling of friendship and leisurely enterprise and comfort the two always found together, whatever the circumstances. In any case, he was concerned about the Rat's health — which was surely much more important than forgetfulness of a birthday! — and he welcomed this opportunity to raise what he knew might be a difficult subject.

"Ratty, dear friend, I was wondering if I might just risk your ire and mention a matter that has worried me concerning your well-being? You have seemed so out of sorts lately."

"Humph!" said the Rat, frowning, for he had no wish to spoil a day that had gone so well with talk of his health.

"No, really, Ratty, if I cannot say what I feel on this subject then who else — ?"

"Mole," said the Rat with sudden and unexpected good humour, "do you not think that one of those excellent chocolate truffles Master Toad thoughtfully brought back from Paris for each of us might just complete an excellent morning's work doing nothing in particular?"

The Mole could not but agree and allow himself to be

diverted for the moment from his purpose. In any case, he and Nephew had long since scoffed all of *their* box whilst the more austere Water Rat appeared to have a good many left.

"Rwatty," he began a little later (the truffles were large, succulent and gooey, and it was not easy to talk and eat one at the same time), "I yam – I dwoo – just a moment, old fwellow."

The Mole chomped away, nodding his head, rolling his eyes, and trying to make his point by gesture alone, but not succeeding very well.

"What I was trying to say," he said at last, "is that you really must try to see some sense on this matter and consult a –"

"Have another, Moly old chap. It'll help you think about the things that *really* matter."

The Mole tried not to accept but – but accept he did.

"Well," he said, "wharr sheems to be impor – impwor – O bwother!"

"Let's leave that subject, shall we?" said the Rat quietly and firmly.

"Yes, Ratty," said the Mole meekly, and together they watched the River's flow. As a light breeze began to make the branches of the willows opposite tremble, they sat in silence, Ratty dwelling upon their happy yesterdays, the Mole pondering a less certain future.

A long time later, as it seemed, the Rat's ship's clock struck half past two, and he announced it was time to take the Mole home.

"It has been a very pleasant morning but the days are drawing in and there's a moist chill in the air. I must get you back if I am to be home myself before dark."

"Yes, Ratty," said the Mole, not yet moving. "Tell me, has the River given you further notice of that warning you sensed some weeks ago?"

"She has," said the Rat quietly. "I was too tired to accompany him myself, but Otter went upstream to the Town the other day, with Young Rat for company, and looked again at those filthy factories we saw."

The Mole nodded grimly at the memory.

"It is not good news, Mole. She looks all right to those who see only the reflections of the sun and sky upon her surface. But those of us who look deeper see that she is sick, and hurt. She is ailing, Mole, and I fear matters will get a great deal worse before they ever get better. I never thought I would be glad to say that I am growing old, or that I do not want to know what the future holds in store. But so it is, so it is."

In this quiet way the Rat intimated to his friend why he had no wish to talk of his health, and that he was as aware as Mole that he was growing old. What did he have to live for if she he loved might already be dying and he unable to do aught about it?

"O Ratty," whispered the Mole.

They sat in silence a few more moments before the Mole roused himself, stretched and said, "I had not intended to mention it but I would like to do so now, and I know you will not take it amiss. Today is my birthday, and I confess I was a little disappointed that you had forgotten it."

"Why, my dear chap, I really, I mean —" cried the Rat, quite genuinely lost for words.

"No, no, do not apologize," said the Mole, raising a hand. "Let me say only that I could think of no better place to spend this day than here, talking just as we have always done. *This* has been my birthday and I am grateful for it. Take me home now, but do not mention what I have said to Nephew, who also forgot. A quiet and modest supper with him and early to bed, that's all I require."

"Well, Mole," replied the Rat, recovering his composure and much amused, "I wonder if you will still say so when you put your head upon your pillow tonight. Meanwhile, I am sorry if –"

"Really, no apologies! Now, boatman, ferry me home!"

Mr Toad's day had started earlier, and had proved a lot less pleasant than Mole and Ratty's.

He had risen early and after a hearty breakfast dressed himself in his hiking gear, except for his jacket, cap and snow goggles. He was taking a turn about his terrace, alpenstock in hand, when Master Toad finally made his first appearance of the day.

Gone was the youth's grand resolution of the night before, and desire to be compliant to Toad's will. Back had come the malingerer, the prevaricator, the maker of excuses – especially when Toad appeared from outside, hale and hearty, and dressed, as it seemed to his ward, in a ridiculous yet intimidating way.

"You cannot mean that I, 'oo 'as 'is clothes fitted by the most chic houses in Paris should wear such monstrosities as these?" he exclaimed.

"Sensible and practical they are," declared Toad, "and you will get used to them."

"What time this afternoon do you propose we go 'iking?" he asked his guardian unenthusiastically. "I am weakening rapidly and before long I fear my knees will not be able to support my weight and regretfully I shall 'ave to rest."

"That *is* a shame," said Toad, "and I would not want to put you to the trouble of climbing stairs in such a state, but I have something I bought specially for you, and have left it in my bed-chamber. But if you are too weak —"

Master Toad, who rather liked gifts and suchlike, rose with alacrity, saying, "Only *later* will I be so weak, but for now —"

With that, and driven by the same greed that afflicts so many indulged youths of the wealthier classes, he scampered up the stairs, two at a time.

A short time later he returned looking crestfallen, carrying the pair of hobnail boots Toad had left out for him, along with a handwritten tag that read: *For Master Toad, on the occasion of his first hike.*

"In view of the fact that weakness will beset you later today," said the ruthless Toad, "and that you still have enough strength in your legs to bound up the stairs, I suggest we leave at once. Finish your breakfast, put on these hiking clothes and report to the gun room!"

"But, Pater," cried the defeated youth. "My studies, my work!"

"Pooh to that!" said Toad. "I'll see you in five minutes."

Master Toad found his guardian ready and waiting, and greatly to his surprise carrying a haversack a great deal larger than the one intended for himself.

"Put that on your back and follow me," said Toad tersely, pointing to the lesser one.

Master Toad grudgingly complied, hoisting the wretched thing onto his back with a curious twisting contortion, and a strangled grunt.

"Where are we going?" he panted as he was led round the corner of the house towards the garden terrace, sweat already breaking out upon his youthful brow.

This seemed a reasonable enough question to ask, but Toad gave it a strange response.

"I want no moaning or grumbling! I want no insubordination! Follow my lead without question and we will get there."

He was following Colonel Wheeler's injunction to leaders not to show their hands too soon to those they lead. That warning had been given lest a leader lose his way and the party become demoralized, but Toad knew perfectly well where he was going. Indeed he was greatly looking forward to reaching Mole End and intended to be there when the surprise birthday party was due to begin — but first he planned to take Master Toad to wilder parts for some instruction in the skills of hiking.

So it was that Toad found himself leading his young and increasingly rebellious ward across his garden, a terrain that till that moment had been perfectly familiar to both of them, but which with loads upon their shoulders suddenly seemed full of steep hills and treacherous hollows, and decidedly alien. To make it worse, for the special occasion of the Mole's birthday Toad had impulsively thrown three bottles of champagne and some cheeses into their haversacks, which weighed them down more than he might have expected.

Toad had decided upon the Wild Wood as the site most suitable for the instruction he intended to give in the arts of mountain navigation, scrambling and rope-work, the techniques of traversing glaciers and climbing sheer ice walls — and other skills Colonel Wheeler deemed it wise for expedition leaders to impart to their followers. That the Wild Wood had no such natural features was rather a relief to the indolent Toad. Yet he felt sure that with a bit of imagination, the large and ancient oak trees would do for the climbing, and the root-veined forest floor would double up for glaciers.

A short while later, they had made their way, with not a little difficulty, over the great hill that was the Iron Bridge, to the edge of the Wild Wood. Then, peering into its dark interior, eyeing its shifting shadows, listening to the eerie sounds from within of the crying and baying of predatory creatures, and the hisses and whispers of sinister ones, Toad immediately had second thoughts. A fact which Master Toad very quickly surmised, suggesting that a walk along the bank in the direction of Ratty's house might serve best to orientate them to the new world of the expeditionary.

"We might 'ave a cup of tea with Mr Ratty," his ward dared suggest.

"Exactly what I had in mind, dear fellow, but I would be obliged if you would leave the leading to me and the following to yourself!" said the self-important Toad, taking the path alongside the Wild Wood, and averting his eyes from its threatening interior.

For a short while their hike became almost pleasant, but all too soon their haversacks grew heavier on their backs once more, and the two adventurers began to find that even this most familiar and normally trouble-free of paths presented unexpected difficulties and dangers. In no time at all Toad had strayed far from the River and found himself among bramble bushes a good deal higher than himself. In consequence he got quite lost, fell into muddy dikes (six times, the same one twice), tripped over his trusty alpenstock (times without number) and finally managed to entangle both of them in his climbing rope in a thicket.

It was as they sat back to back, struggling to free themselves, that a cloud obscured the sun, all suddenly grew gloomy and Toad realized how far they had strayed into the Wild Wood. The brambles of the River Bank had been left far behind, and were replaced now by the twists and contortions of old yew trees and bent beech, amongst which the more ancient trees of oak and elm, which it had been his original intention to utilize for climbing practice, rose up like malevolent giants.

A chill wind seemed to blow up from nowhere, even as those shrieks and cries, those shifting sounds and shadowy forms that they had been seeking to avoid all morning, redoubled in intensity.

"Toad!" whispered a voice from a nearby thicket.

"Ha! Ha! Ha!" mocked another voice from amongst the rotting branches of a fallen tree, where Toad was sure he espied the blinking of black shiny eyes and the glint of sharp teeth.

Then, in a lower whining weaselly-stoatish kind of voice, "Young toads, we like 'em: we marinate 'em, we roast 'em and eat 'em up! Ha! Ha! Ha!"

Whether or not Toad heard this last was doubtful for he was already in a blind panic, but Master Toad heard the threats, or thought he did, and cried, "Mr Toad, what shall we do? We are lost! We shall die! They will 'ave us for tea!"

Not for the first time since he had assumed his wardship of Master Toad, Toad discovered in himself resources he did not know he had.

It was perfectly true that a moment before his thoughts had been only of himself and his desire to escape as he struggled to free himself from the clinging ropes and the clutching branches all about. But when he heard Master Toad's plaintive cry and pathetic sobs, the guardian heart of Toad was touched, and some nascent

parental urge to help one weaker than himself and in his care was released. Remembering that Colonel Wheeler had recommended that a vicious hunting knife be packed in one of the outside pockets of the haversack, he retrieved it and swiftly cut loose their bonds, and in great and savage sweeps hewed down the branches that imprisoned them.

Then with wild cries, and waving his alpenstock about his head, he drove the close circle of weasel eyes and stoat teeth back, and hauled the trembling and weeping Master Toad to his feet.

"Follow me!" he yelled and, grabbing Master Toad's lapel that he might not lose him, he began to flee in what he trusted was the direction of the River. Yet after only a few minutes his Viking spirit began to flag, and he gasped for breath as he heard the creatures of the Wild Wood following fast in the shadows, calling and hissing, whistling and mocking.

"Where are we going?" wailed Master Toad. "Is 'iking in the country always so *dangereux*?"

How mortally afraid he must be to be slipping back so swiftly into his native tongue!

"*Mon dieu!*" he cried. "Look there!"

The weasels and stoats were closing in fast and even as Toad and his ward were greeted by the welcome sight of the River Bank once more, their path was blocked by the massed ranks of the enemy, carrying weapons of all kinds, and, like some heathen New Guinea tribe, ready now to hew their victims down. The villains began to advance upon them with terrible cries.

Retreating along the bank, with his ward clinging

around his neck, Toad was about to offer his old enemies all he possessed, including Toad Hall itself, in exchange for their lives, when he stumbled across something he had not touched or seen in many a long year. Something he had quite forgotten existed.

It was the entrance to the tunnel that Badger had first revealed to him on that most memorable evening when he and Toad, along with Ratty and Mole, had successfully wrested back Toad Hall from the fathers and grandfathers of these same villainous weasels and stoats who had ambushed them now. Hewn many hundreds of years before, it had been turned by Toad's father into a secret passage between the River Bank and Toad Hall, no doubt as a possible escape route from pressing creditors and the like. Now it offered his son quick and safe passage back to the safety of his own home.

Pushing Master Toad through into the echoing darkness, Toad swiftly blocked the opening with boulders and other such rubbish, even as his ward prodded at the enemy to keep them at bay. Then, opening another of the pouches of his haversack, he produced matches and a taper, with which he had planned to light their campfire. Now it served as a torch to light their escape along the dark, damp, narrow passage. With the thwarted weasels and stoats receding behind them, the two toads fled up the tunnel, putting obstacles in the way as they went, till finally, with a push and a shove at the trap-door, they tumbled headlong into the kitchens of the Hall.

This caused three kitchen maids to faint, and the boot-boy to flee, leaving only the Cook to belabour them with a soup ladle before she realized who they were.

No matter of that! Having securely battened down the trap-door and placed several sacks of flour on top, just to make certain, they were safe – and food and drink were readily to hand to help them recover their sanity and strength.

"You know, Master Toad," said Toad a good deal later – they sat at the kitchen table, still in their hiking gear, with the servants having joined them in their fare so that their eccentric master might have an audience for his tale of how the weasels and stoats were fooled and duped by the superior cunning and intelligence of toads – "I think that we should now adjourn to the terrace, and thence by way of paths familiar, to Mole End, where Mole is to celebrate his birthday this afternoon."

"Lor', sir," said the Cook, "the arternoon's nearly over for it's nigh on five o'clock. That's the servants' supper you've been eating for your lunch!"

"How swiftly time passes by for those engaged in heroes' work!" cried Toad, rising. "Come, Master Toad, to Mole End at once – and don't forget those haversacks, for we have champagne to deliver and more tales to tell!"

Thus persuaded, and now rather looking forward to showing off to Toad's friends, Master Toad followed his guardian into the open air once more, only tiring when they saw the lights of Mole End across a field.

"We shall soon be there?" he asked, for lights at dusk have a strange way of receding.

"We shall!" cried Toad, "and you can take it from me that we will receive a right royal welcome!"

* * *

Mole's birthday party had gone without a hitch, just as the Rat had hoped it might. Nephew had done all the preparatory work at Mole End and the Mole had arrived back to find a huge banner across the front of his home that read: "HAPPY BIRTHDAY, MOLE & MANY MORE TO COME!!!" Whilst from every window latch, door handle, and hook or nail in the wall, outside and in, hung clusters of balloons and ribbons. Best of all, Portly, Grandson, as well as Nephew, were all there to shake his hand and greet him.

"Happy Birthday, Mole old fellow!" cried the Rat, who was almost as overwhelmed by the good work of Nephew and his friends as the Mole himself.

"But −" he began.

"You said −" he continued.

"Ratty, I thought −" he protested.

"O my," he whispered as they all clustered about him and sang "Happy Birthday to You".

Ready laughter mixed with tears of happiness as he turned first to the Rat, then to Nephew, then to each of the others, not knowing what to say or whom to thank. "O my, I surely don't deserve it," said he, wiping the tears from his eyes, yet sobbing still.

"You deserve it and a great deal more, and we all think so," said the Rat. "And Mr Badger thinks so too. He has sent a special card apologizing for his absence, as he and Otter have had to go to the Town on urgent River business. It seems there is some talk in the Town of building new houses in the Wild Wood that must be nipped in the bud."

"Badger sent *me* a card!" said the Mole, more interested

just then in present pleasures than in future threats.

"And Mr Toad told us," continued Nephew, "that though he was otherwise engaged with Master Toad this afternoon he would make every effort to see that the two of them join us a little later, and that he will bring the champagne with him."

"Toad bringing me champagne!"

"Now come on, Mole," said the Rat, the others having agreed he should be Master of Ceremonies, "come inside and tuck into the birthday tea we have prepared."

"Tea? For me? O dear, I am going to cry again."

But how truly happy he was that afternoon, and happier still as the afternoon progressed and dusk came. Indeed, everything seemed perfect – and might have stayed so, had not Portly and Nephew gone outside for a breath of fresh air, only to come rushing back in a state of alarm.

"Uncle! You others! Keep quiet!"

"Why, what is it?" cried the Rat, rising from his seat in alarm.

"The Beast's out there and he's coming this way!" whispered Nephew.

"The Beast?" said the Rat louder than he should.

"But there is no Beast," said the stalwart Mole.

"There is, and we've just seen him clambering over the gate," said Portly.

"But – but –" began the Mole.

"Shhh! Mole, old fellow," commanded the Rat. "I can see these two mean business, so the least we can do is to investigate their claims."

He crept to a window and peered out.

"Good heavens," he whispered, aghast, "we must arm ourselves."

"Why, what can you see?" said the Mole, joining the Rat, and peering out from a now darkened Mole End.

"Them!" said the Rat very grimly indeed, pointing a finger through the dusk.

It was true. Out of the darkness came two figures, hunch-backed and shambling as primeval creatures do, stopping now and then to look about, and the bigger one, the leader, holding an enormous stave.

"The Beast and his Mate!" said the Rat.

The front door was still ajar and as the Rat went to close and bolt it they heard the most terrible grunting and groaning coming from the beasts, and then strange other-worldly mutterings.

"See how their eyes stare so horribly!" whispered Portly from the window, for as on previous sightings the creatures seemed to have great white ovoid eyes.

The Mole, who had recovered himself and taken up the trusty cudgel that had stood him so well in the past in crises such as these, was now calm determination itself, and said, "They seem big, and they certainly sound dangerous, but there are five of us and only two of –"

"They're advancing once again," said Portly.

"What do you think we should do?" said the Mole tersely.

"Surprise is always the best form of attack," answered Grandson stoutly. "Have you perhaps any other weapons so that as they reach the door we can spring it open, charge them down, and overpower them?"

Thus it was that as the Beast's grunting and groaning outside began once more, and there came a primordial knocking and clattering at the door, the Rat let forth his battle cry, *"Charge them down, and give no quarter to our enemy!"*

As the door burst open, the two exhausted, startled figures on the doorstep were sent flying, landing in a tangled heap of arms and legs and straps.

"Look, the Beast has four legs!" cried Grandson, not realizing who owned the limbs he was now attacking.

"The Beast wears khaki-coloured armour to protect itself!" cried the Mole, bringing down his cudgel a good many times on the haversacks.

"Destroy the Beast!" cried Nephew, upon whom a Viking-like frenzy had fallen. While Young Rat prepared to offer the coup de grace with his marlin spike.

No, it had certainly not been a good day for Toad. An enterprise that had seemed so sensible and foolproof, so well planned and so full of promise, had gone from difficulty to disaster and from disaster to this sudden and unprovoked attack from an enemy Toad could not see, for his goggles had misted up once more, and anyway his aggressor could not be anyone he knew.

Heaving himself to the vertical with his alpenstock, he roared, "Seek to assault two innocent hikers out for a day's stroll and about to visit their harmless and law-abiding friends, would you? Imagine that you could hurt and destroy Toad of Toad Hall, eh?"

Then he counter-attacked, venting his spleen upon his attackers for the tribulations and frustrations of the day. As he began his assault a similar passion overcame the still-fallen Master Toad, suffused with a determination to be vanquished no more, and appalled at seeing his pater so unfairly attacked.

Casting off his haversack at last, and hauling off his loathsome hobnail boots that they might be used in his attack, he began to fight side by side with Toad.

"But it's Toad of Toad Hall!" cried the Mole, when he saw at last who it was they had attacked, and who was counter-attacking with very formidable might and determination.

"*And* Master Toad," cried Nephew, in astonishment.

"Toad, it's only *us!*" yelled the Rat when he realized their mistake.

For a moment Toad paused as they retreated towards the Mole's house before his counter-attack, and suddenly he recognized his attackers.

"Toad, we're sorry – we thought you were the Beast!" cried Mole.

For Toad, still reeling from the humiliation and

outrage of their assault a moment before, and the pain of their blows upon his legs, this was the final straw.

"What impudence!" exploded Toad. "How could you possibly mistake the great and handsome Toad of Toad Hall for the hideous Beast of the Iron Bridge?! Why, I've never heard such cheek!

"Khaki-coloured armour, eh?" he yelled, shoving the contrite Mole back through his own front door.

"A beast with four legs, am I?" he roared, setting about Grandson with a will.

"Invited for tea, are we?" he screeched, raising his alpenstock once more.

"You most certainly are," said Nephew calmly and soothingly, staying Toad's hand, "and I am sure we have some delectable fruit cake which Ratty made only yesterday evening."

"Hmm. Fruit cake, you say?" said Toad faintly, before turning to Master Toad and asking, "Shall we destroy them all and raze Mole End to the ground, young Master Toad . . . or join them for tea?"

"I do hope you'll decide upon the latter course," called out Ratty from behind the Mole's dresser, to where he had felt it wisest to retreat in a quite uncharacteristic display of cowardice, but then he had never confronted an enemy quite so – so absolute – as Toad that day, "for that champagne you so kindly offered to bring will be most welcome."

"And we can find you a Havana cigar as well," offered the Mole, emerging from behind the kitchen door, where he had felt it best to take refuge.

"Hmmm!" grunted Toad, sitting down and accepting the cake that Nephew offered him.

"Well!" he growled a little later, sipping the champagne now opened and poured.

"Mmmm!" he muttered, as he contemplated the Havana and put it down ready for use.

No, it had not been Toad's day – till now. For he never was an animal to hold grudges, and was always willing to laugh at himself and see to it that others around him were happy and well set, once he had had a little of his own way.

"Well, and what do you think, Master Toad," said he finally, with a twinkle in his eye, "that a toad should do when after such a hard day's work as we have had he is beaten and insulted by his hosts?"

The company fell silent, waiting upon Master Toad's response.

"Well, Pater –" he began, but then he paused, for he thought that perhaps this was the final test of one who has been tried all day in the disciplines of educational exercise, and that much might depend upon the nature and quality of his reply.

"I think, possibly," he continued, raising his glass, "that it would be a very good idea if we wished Mole a very happy birthday, and *you* made a speech!"

If there was a moment when Master Toad was finally accepted into River Bank society absolutely and without question, a moment that suggested that he had those same inestimable qualities that Toad had in such abundance, and which allowed others to forgive so very much, that was it.

"A speech?" said Toad, rising like a fish to bait.

"At once, Toad," said the Rat.

"Upon the subject of Mole's birthday, and why we are assembled here today to celebrate it?"

"Yes please, Mr Toad," said Nephew.

"Master Toad, hand me my haversack!"

"It just happens," said the incorrigible Toad, fumbling from one pocket of the haversack to another before he found what he wanted, "that I have a speech prepared on that very subject!"

Very much later, when all the drink was nearly drunk, and all the food nearly eaten, and night had come, the Mole asked Toad and Master Toad what they had been doing all day, "if it is not presumptuous to ask?"

"Doing?" cried the irrepressible Toad with spirit. "Why we were partaking of the very latest, and the very best, form of exercise."

"Labouring with heavy loads?" said the perplexed Mole, eyeing the enormous haversacks.

"We were hiking," said Toad, "and don't worry about the size of that haversack, Mole old chap. You'll work up to it in time? Eh, Master Toad?"

"'E will, I expect," came the reply.

"But do you enjoy it?"

"Wonderful!" said Toad, taking up some fruit cake. "Eh, Master Toad?"

Had those others present known something of the history of the day they might have noticed a momentary pause before Toad's ward replied, during which a silent struggle took place between that youth's natural desire to say how truly awful hiking was and his toadish inclination to impress all with his strengths and abilities, and modishness.

"Nothing better than 'iking!" he declared at last, scoffing a last crumb of cake and basking in the admiration of his peers.

·VI·
A Touch of Araby

November came, and with it a sudden and unseasonable sweep of blizzard snow from the north, which blanked out the River Bank, and draped the trees of the Wild Wood with hoarfrost, heralding a hard and bitter winter.

It was a time to stay indoors and enjoy the comforts of home, be they food, friendship or fond memory. Or, if an animal *must* go out, a time to wrap up well and finish daytime chores before the freezing shadows of the night return, unless it be to visit friends and there find comfort by the fireside, and companionable conversations about times gone by, and thoughts and hopes of spring.

The Mole's growing concern about the Rat's well-being seemed to find confirmation when, a week after the snow had thawed and the last pockets of ice were melting, he and Nephew, who had taken advantage of the brief spell of milder weather to go out for a brisk walk, came home to find a most alarming note pinned to their door at Mole End in an unfamiliar hand.

The Mole glanced quickly at the signature and ascertained it was from Young Rat, but its untidy scrawl seemed so out of character that the Mole guessed it had been written in some haste.

"Dear Mr Mole! It's the Cap'n, sir," he read, realizing it was Ratty who was referred to, *"he's gone poorly and you had better come as soon as you can."*

"What ever can this mean, Nephew," said the Mole with a worried frown.

Nephew looked at the note and said, "I expect Ratty has simply caught a cold or something, and that what is needed is one of your herbal remedies."

But no sooner had they begun to delve into Mole's cupboards for those healing balms and cures he took such pride in, than Young Rat himself appeared from the direction of the River.

"Mr Badger sent me to see if you were back," he cried. "Mr Ratty's failing fast!"

"O my!" cried the Mole wildly. "O *my*! Whatever's wrong with him?"

"The doctor says he may not last the night," said Young Rat, hopping about from one foot to the other, and clearly quite as flummoxed as the Mole, "so hurry and come quick!"

Nephew bundled his uncle back into coat and boots and thrust into a bag some remedies and healing balms. Then they all set off on the path down towards the River and the Rat's House, but in such haste and dismay that they forgot even to close the door of Mole End behind them, which was left open to the winter wind.

On the way Nephew managed to elicit from Young Rat an account of what had happened. It seemed that last night he and the Rat had spent a quiet and pleasant evening together and gone early to their beds soon after dinner, the night being cold. Early the next morning, the Otter and Portly had called on them, but Ratty had declined to join them on their outing, the recent wintry weather having brought on one or two aches and pains. Apart from those, however, Ratty had been well when Young Rat had left that morning.

Nevertheless, Young Rat had not felt quite happy after he had left his friend and mentor alone, and somehow there was something in the River's flow, in the swirling of its dark pools, in the shadows of its further banks, that made him ask the Otter if he could hurry home.

"What is it that worries you?" the Otter had said.

"Not sure, don't know, the River. Shouldn't be here – it's Cap'n Ratty, I think he's in trouble."

Otter needed no second telling, for he had learnt in the months past that Young Rat's communion with the River was every bit as acute and reliable as Ratty's own. In any case, the River *had* seemed strange that day and more so as the morning advanced.

So the Otter and Portly had accompanied Young Rat

back home at once, and there were met by a sight far more alarming than their worst forebodings. Poor Ratty lay groaning upon the floor, fragments of coal about him, evidence that he had been in the act of refuelling the fire when he was stricken down. Now the fire had gone out, the room grown cold, and Ratty was half incoherent with pains about his chest and arms.

The Otter had taken charge at once – sending Young Rat to fetch Mole, for in such cases his services were invaluable, and sending Portly to fetch the Badger, and at the same time send for a doctor. These errands done, and the Mole being absent from Mole End, the others had stayed by the Rat and helped him as they might.

"After the doctor came Badger told me to hurry back to Mole End, sir," concluded Young Rat, before expertly berthing the boat at the Rat's landing stage and helping the Mole and Nephew disembark. "He said you know Ratty better than any doctor and might help find out what ails him."

The scene that met their gaze when they entered the Rat's parlour confirmed their worst fears. The room had the pungent odour of acerbic ointments and medicine. Otter was there leaning against the mantelpiece, shaking his head; Portly as well, but sitting slumped by the fireside in which the few flames of a paltry fire guttered and struggled for life.

The Badger loomed at the Rat's bedroom door. With an instruction to Nephew to tend to the fire, the Mole peered past the Badger towards the Rat's bed, where he espied a gentleman in a dark suit, with a doctor's valise open at his feet as he sat at the Rat's side, holding his wrist and studying his pocket watch with a worried frown.

"He's very near the end, I fear," whispered the Badger.

"The end?" gasped the Mole.

As if to confirm the fact, the doctor rose, placed the Rat's unresisting hand back upon his chest, and with much frowning and shaking of his head retreated from the room, signalling the Badger to come with him that they might talk.

"But what's happened?" demanded Mole, anxious to go at once to Ratty's side.

The Badger quickly introduced him to the doctor, who was of the tall, whiskery, cadaverous kind, who regard their patients as nuisances, and the Mole was invited to join their hushed consultation.

"The symptoms are grave indeed," pronounced the doctor, "and I fear —"

"But surely he is not — he is not going to — ?" cried poor Mole, quite beside himself.

"It is a wonder he has clung on so well," said the doctor wearily, giving the impression that it had been rather unreasonable of the Rat to have done so and thus prolong the agony (for his friends) and inconvenience of a country call (for the doctor), "for with so faint a pulse, and loss of all sensibilities apart from the power of hearing, which is often the last to go, I would not have thought that he would have survived this morning, when I believe he was first found."

"If only we had been in when Young Rat first came!" cried the Mole in much distress. "I might then have brought him some herbal tea, or a poultice perhaps, and then, then —"

126

"Tut tut, sir!" said the doctor with some asperity. "One so gravely ill as Mr Rat would hardly respond to tea and sympathy if he has not responded to my best efforts for the last three hours. I very strongly suggest, indeed I absolutely insist, that my patient should not be troubled with old woman's remedies, nor forcibly given liquids, for in his condition . . . In any case, he is drifting in and out of sleep now, and has mumbled a few words, so perhaps I have averted the crisis and he will make some kind of recovery, even if it is too much to expect him ever to lead an active life again."

"Ratty inactive!" cried the Mole. "No, that cannot be. Please be so good as to tell me what is *wrong* with him?"

His dander was up, for domesticated he might be, but "old woman" he was not, and he had never forced Ratty to do anything in his life except – except –

Mole felt a sudden pang then, a brief and troubling memory of a time when he *had* forced Ratty to do something. Why, if Ratty did not recover, then he would never be able to follow the dream that the Mole had dissuaded him from following so many years before.

"O my!" he said aloud, sobbing suddenly. "If only Ratty would survive I swear I shall never make him do anything he does not want to do, or stand in his way!"

"Why, Mole, whatever can you mean?" said the Badger.

But this moment of weakness and doubt on the Mole's part passed as suddenly and mysteriously as it had come and, taking a grip upon himself, he stood upright once more and stared boldly in the doctor's eye, for his earlier question had not been answered, and they could do nothing useful till it had.

"What is wrong with my friend?" he asked once more.

"*Wrong* with him?" said the doctor guardedly.

"Yes," said the Badger, glad of the Mole's question. "You have been treating him for half the day; surely you have come to some conclusion or other?"

"What is *wrong* with him is very plain," said the doctor brusquely, though the Rat's friends fancied they detected a touch of uncertainty beneath his now chilly air. "He is suffering from that form of physical dementia of which a general paralysis of the vital organs and nervous functions is the most marked symptom, and for which the only known cure is extreme rest, an abstinence from violent exertion and sudden shocks – either of which might cause a complete collapse and both of which certainly would – and, if the condition worsens further still, then as a last resort the application of steam heat to loosen the blood, followed by leeches to release it entirely."

"Steam heat?" whispered the Mole, who knew that the Rat did not much like hot and humid days.

"Leeches?" muttered the Badger, who had early memories of those loathsome creatures being applied to his maiden aunt to cure a persistent cough, and her rapid demise very soon afterwards.

"Just so," said the doctor. "I shall be back tomorrow morning to reexamine the patient, and meanwhile, though I have desisted from giving him medicine till now, you might give him these pills. My bill will be in the post."

His face creased into an ambiguous and not entirely pleasant smile, and then he was gone into the twilight without a further glance at his patient.

If the Mole had been in a state of shock till now, and slow to respond to the crisis, he quickly recovered himself after the doctor's departure.

"Old woman, am I? Steam heat indeed! Leeches, my foot! Let me take a look at Ratty for myself before we give him any of this doctor's pills!" Then he paused and said, "Did the doctor say he had given Ratty no medicine at all?"

"None that I have seen," said the Badger.

The Mole sniffed the air and said, "But I thought I caught the smell of medicine when we arrived, or of an ointment of some kind."

Then, ignoring all the Badger's protestations, Mole suggested that Young Rat should stand by to ferry him across the River to Mole End for temporary bedding and certain supplies that he might stay the night. Then, when he had ordered Portly to fetch more fuel for the fire, and instructed Nephew to tidy up the kitchen while he was at it, for it seemed to be in an awful mess, he went at last to the Rat's side.

"My dear chap," he began, taking his friend's hand in his own.

Ratty let forth a faint moan.

"Can you hear me?"

He managed a feeble groan.

"Can you tell me where it hurts?"

The fingers of the Rat's other hand fluttered about the counterpane as if to indicate the concept of "all over".

"That is not much use to me, Ratty," said the Mole firmly, "so will you please be more particular?"

The Rat frowned and allowed his free hand to settle finally upon his stomach.

"You have pains especially there?" said the Mole. *"Here?"* As the Badger watched, the Mole pressed the Rat's stomach gently and his friend managed both a moan and a groan, and then tried to speak.

"He seems to be trying to say something," said the Badger.

"And his eyes are opening," said the Mole, "which is a hopeful sign."

They did open and he spoke, though not in a way that seemed to make much sense.

"It was very nice," he said.

The Badger frowned and glanced at the Mole.

"What was very nice, old fellow?" asked Mole.

"Never known the like before! A touch of Araby! It was almost worth it."

"Araby?" whispered the Mole, returning the Badger's glance and mutely sharing that wise animal's sad opinion that the Rat's dementia was worsening.

The Rat then broke into a strange and plaintive hum, waving his hands about and rolling his eyes.

"They do it in the souks, he said."

"Ratty, dear chap," said the Mole very gently, "why do you not try to get more sleep?"

"Is there any left?" asked the Rat, breaking into his strange other-world hum once more and turning on his side away from them both before he added sleepily. "Because if there is you should try some, Moly. Please

do not take offence if I say it tastes quite the equal of your fennel and ramson stew."

A slow dawning light came to the Mole's eyes and he stood up, leaned over the Rat and asked, "What did you eat last evening?"

"And quite as good as your quince and mulberry parfait, old chap, yes we –"

"Ratty, wake up at once!"

But the Rat was asleep, his crisis fading fast, and with a look of blissful memory upon his face.

"It's something he has eaten!" pronounced the Mole grimly. "I have seen Ratty in a similar condition before, after he had eaten my wild mushroom and broccoli pie with stewed cucumber and cauliflower sauce."

"But that's one of your best autumn dishes," said the Badger.

"It may be to you and me, but I am afraid it gives Ratty indigestion," said the Mole. "This talk of Araby and suchlike suggests that Young Rat has been trying his hand at some cooking of a kind too exotic and spicy for Ratty."

Young Rat appeared, and confirmed that he had indeed cooked for the Rat the evening before.

"Did so at the Cap'n's request," said the youngster. "Told 'im I had a mind to try my hand in the galley, seeing as we've had a bit too much of his stickleback and potato pie lately, not to mention his baked pike in chutney and roach and ramson mulch.

"Ratty didn't take it wrong, and warmed to my tales of Pa's cooking in the old days, especially after he had served a spell as stoker in the kitchen of the Caliph of Al

Basrah. The Cap'n was taken with my songs and tales of those parts and said to surprise him with some dishes of the East."

"O Ratty!" groaned the Mole, as if the stricken animal were at his side. "You know that rich and exotic food does not agree with you!"

"Well, anyway, when Mr Otter took me to the Town a week ago I bought some ingredients from a sailor's shop that caters for mariners who miss the foods of Araby, as I do, and beginning last week I took my turn in the galley. We started with mogul crayfish with Malayan banana-bean sauce —"

"Crayfish, Nephew, he gave poor Ratty *crayfish*!"

"In bean sauce, Uncle. That cannot have helped at all!"

"— then he was much taken with my version of Pa's Shaljamiya Chicken."

"Which is?"

"Chicken drowned in turnip and goat's cheese stew."

"Turnip! O my! O dear!"

"But it was the Cairo crab he really liked, served with aubergines lightly fried in sesame oil with turmeric and bodi onions."

"Crab! Aubergines! Bodi onions!" cried the Mole distractedly.

"Raw," said the indefatigable and foolish Young Rat.

The Mole had heard quite enough and went back into Ratty's room and stood over his bed.

"Ratty, wake up at once!" he cried.

Reluctantly, sheepishly, the Rat opened his eyes.

"Is it any wonder," pronounced the Mole very severely, "that you have been so ill after persuading

Young Rat, who knew no better, to cook such dangerous concoctions for you?"

"But they weren't concoctions, Mole, they were deli-
cious, every one, though perhaps I ate overmuch of one
or two of them."

"Of all of them, I rather fear," said the Mole.

"But their scents, Mole, they were mouth-wateringly
wonderful! How could I refuse? And they conjured up
for me, more than anything I have known in the years
since he so briefly visited the River Bank, that far-off
world evoked for me when Young Rat's father, the Sea
Rat, came to the River Bank. O, how I wish I had
followed my whim and visited those places of which he
spoke. Young Rat, sing him one of the songs your father
learnt in the Caliph's harem!"

As Young Rat essayed to do so, his voice rising and
falling with the strange cadences of the East, the Rat
managed at last to sit up, and waved his hands about as if
conducting his assistant's song.

"Do you remember the Sea Rat?" asked the Rat
dreamily.

"I do. O, I do," said the Mole, for it was that same Sea
Rat whose stories of Araby and the Orient had so nearly
seduced the Rat into leaving them. "O my! O my!" said
the Mole miserably, sitting down on Ratty's bed.

"Whatever is it, old fellow?" said the Rat.

"When you were so ill just now, and I thought you
might not pull through, well, I thought, though it was
silly of me, that you —"

"There, there, Mole, don't take on so. What did you
think?"

"I remembered how I stopped you from following the Sea Rat on his travels, which I since have often thought I had no right to do, and I told myself that if you recovered I would never again dare suggest you should not follow that desire for travel and exploration in exotic realms that you have felt for so long!"

The affection in which the two held each other was well known, but there are occasions when the truth is more important, and so far as the Rat was concerned this was one of them. For he did not now seek to reassure the Mole, indeed he went so far as to remove his hand from his friend's, and his eyes hardened a little.

"Mole, old fellow, you have dared raise a subject I have often thought of raising with you. It is perfectly true that but for your intervention I would have followed the Sea Rat south all those long years ago, and our lives might have been very different. I make no complaint about that, for nobody knows better than you how content and fulfilled my life along the River Bank has been — and all the happier and satisfying for your constant companionship.

"Yet, I do not deny that there have been times when I have been regretful — more than regretful perhaps — of that opportunity never taken, a feeling that has grown more rather than less troubling in recent years, especially since Young Rat appeared on the scene. He means no harm with his tales of Araby and the Orient, and gives me pleasure with his songs and his food — even if the after effects are sometimes more than disagreeable! — and he cannot know how wide was that door upon a new and exciting world opened by his father so many years ago, and how I have never quite been able to close it."

The Mole's head slumped lower still.

"Indeed, Mole," cried the Rat passionately, sitting up, brightness returning to his eyes, "do you remember – ?"

Then he realized that others were in the room and perhaps this was not a topic upon which his friend desired a public airing.

"I say, Badger, would you be so kind as to ask Young Rat or Nephew to brew us a nice cup of tea?"

The Badger understood at once and retreated, saying as he closed the door behind him that he would bring in the tea himself.

"Do I remember what?" said the Mole quietly.

"You've probably quite forgotten, but many years ago, when we first met, we were sauntering near Mole End, after you had abandoned it to spend the summer months in my house, and you caught the scent of it, the feeling of it."

"I remember," said the Mole, peering out of the bedroom window across to his own side of the River.

"And do you remember how you had to insist that I listen to you, and that you followed your heart back home?"

"I do, Ratty."

"I was insensitive, was I not?"

"A little, but you quickly made amends."

"Well, Mole, my yearning for foreign climes, my dreams of travel and my desire to journey to those places the Sea Rat and his son once knew so well run very deep – as deep in their own way as that desire for home you felt those long years ago, and still feel. The desire for travel is in the nature of those who lead a nautical life."

"And I denied it you!" cried the Mole brokenly. "It is I who have been insensitive all these years!"

"Why do you think I have kept myself so busy at my River work if not to forget the wanderlust within me? Why do I grow irritable sometimes, especially when autumn comes and I see all those birds migrating, heading off on journeys I myself will now never make?"

"But Ratty, if you really wanted to, then surely you could?"

"No, Mole, not any more. I am too old to follow my youthful dreams, too lacking in energy and enterprise, and I shall never be able to now. And she who has sustained me so long is dying day by day and soon I shall have nothing left, and no hope!"

The Rat could not continue, but only stared out through the window as the Mole had done, at the grey River and the dull wintry scene beyond, as tears of grief for his lost youth coursed unhindered down his face.

"O Ratty, please don't!"

The door quietly opened and the Badger came in with two steaming mugs of tea. He saw at once how things lay, and when the Rat said, "Leave me alone now, please let me be alone!" he understood that it was for the best. There are times when an animal needs solitude.

"Come on, Mole old chap, I expect Ratty could do with some rest once he's drunk his tea – and when he has then I'm sure he'd be glad if you would prepare something for him to eat, something bland and gentle, which will not unsettle him once more."

"Yes, yes, I need to sleep," said the Rat, not looking at either of them but staring out of the window.

So there they left him, the door quietly closed once more, with the Mole very much subdued and overcome by the revelations his friend had made.

"I'm sorry –" began Young Rat, who felt the crisis must be all his fault.

"There is nothing to be sorry for," said the Mole comfortingly, "indeed rather the opposite, for Ratty and I have been made to talk of things too long unsaid and if a friendship is true it should not balk at doing so. Is that not so, Badger?"

The Badger nodded sagely. Then he said, "We have all had enough excitement for one day and I shall go home, and you should do so as well, Nephew, for your uncle and Young Rat here are quite capable of seeing to his needs. I am sure that Ratty will thank Otter and Portly for their help when he is better, but for now –"

"I shall stay here tonight," said the Mole as Nephew and the others dispersed and Young Rat went out with them to help them on their way. Then he stoked the fire, listened for a moment at the Rat's door and, after examining the books upon the Rat's dresser, took down his atlas of the world.

How well thumbed it was, how readily it opened at those central pages that showed the Mediterranean lands. How the Mole sighed as he cast his eyes over all the many names Ratty had underlined over the years: Tangier, Tunis and Syracuse; Crete and Cyprus, Egypt and the Lebanon.

Then, a good many pages on, he found a torn slip of paper marking the pages entitled "The Middle East: Asia, South". Upon that sheet, written not only in the Rat's hand but in Young Rat's too, were those places to which the two had undertaken a culinary journey the night before with such dire consequences: Suez, the Gulf of Aden, and Al Basrah in the Persian Gulf; Bombay, and further off yet, Penang and Kuala Lumpur.

It seemed that the Rat had as yet marked off only one of these destinations on the map itself, this time in red and recently so, for the crayon he had used lay still upon the dresser: Al Basrah, in the kitchen of whose Caliph the Sea Rat once worked, and whose superlative Shaljamiya Chicken had given the Rat so much pleasure – and discomfort.

Yet not a discomfort so great as the Mole felt as he saw what the Rat had written on the paper below this list of names: *"Places I would have liked to visit but now never shall."*

"O my, how wrong I was to make Ratty stay at home, how wrong!" cried the Mole disconsolately, throwing himself down into the Rat's chair and staring at the fire, the atlas open in his hands.

Which is how Young Rat found him when he returned a short time later.

"Mr Mole, are you all right?" asked the youngster.

"No, I am not and nor is Ratty. I am hungry, for I have barely eaten all day, and as for Ratty, I venture to suggest that his appetite will return when he wakes up. Therefore, I would be much obliged if you would set to in the galley and prepare something, for I am too tired and upset to do it myself."

"I could make you the stickleback pie you both like."

"No, I think something a little more – interesting."

"Well then, I suppose I could do coddled eggs – that's a favourite of Mr Ratty's, or used to be before – before –"

"Quite so," said the Mole, "quite so. But I was thinking that perhaps my cooking has been a little unadventurous of late and that if you could find some exotic yet mild dish, one fit for stomachs used to River Bank food yet in need of appetizing excitement —"

"My Pa used to make *rendang daging* for those who have been ill and indisposed, and I think I have the ingredients."

"A raging den gang?" repeated the Mole doubtfully.

"No, *rendang daging* — it's Malayan and means —"

"Pray, do not tell me what it means, or what it contains. Does it perchance come from the environs of Penang?"

"More or less, give or take a few days up a jungle creek in a boat."

"Then please make it for us."

"Of course," said Young Rat. Then he set to with a will, only later adding that it might be wise to have some sweetmeats to follow.

"Sweetmeats," murmured the Mole dreamily, having resumed his perusal of Ratty's atlas and paused awhile in the Persian Gulf. "What is it you have in mind?"

"There's *hais*, of which I have a stock in the larder, for they keep well. Then there's honeyed dates, of which the Caliph himself was especially fond, and of which my Pa became a master when he took over the job of Chief Taster to the Court —"

The Mole waved his hand airily and said, "They sound just the ticket, and I am sure they will help the Rat feel a lot better. But *do* avoid turnips, aubergines and banana-bean sauce, for at least a day or two, if you *don't* mind!"

141

· VII ·
The Uninvited Guest

In the days and weeks following the Rat's sudden indisposition grey mists hung almost continually over the fields and dikes about the River, and the days grew dull and tedious. It was not yet as cold as that sudden snap of ice and snow at the start of November, but the feeling persisted that winter would show its harsher face again before too long.

That the Rat's sudden and alarming "illness" had proved to be nothing more than a severe bout of indigestion brought on by Young Rat's exotic cuisine was naturally a source of some amusement up and down the River Bank.

The Mole was not so easily fooled, however, nor sanguine about those matters which in his hours of greatest discomfort the Rat had so frankly raised.

In any case, the Rat did not recover quite so well as might have been hoped, as if his gastric trials and tribulations had brought out into the open a deeper lassitude and despondency. He tried to seem cheerful and to keep busy, but he did so without much will, and many a time the Mole caught him staring at the River sadly, wistful for past dreams he felt he could not recover, and filled with foreboding for the future of the River he loved so much.

Feeling somewhat responsible for the Rat's malaise and disappointment in his life, the Mole took to spending two or three nights each week at Ratty's home, hoping in that way to raise his spirits, or at least make sure that he did not plunge to yet gloomier depths. In this endeavour he was encouraged by the Rat himself, who asked that he stay close, and who always perked up when, after an absence necessitated by his chores at Mole End, his friend appeared on the far side of the River once more.

"Young Rat, stir yourself and fetch Mole over here, for he must not be kept waiting in the cold!"

Which was all very well, as the Mole observed to Nephew, except that in former days the Rat would have stirred *himself* to be the ferryman. So, after all, decided Mole, Ratty was really *not* himself, and whether it was the advance of years, the decline of the River, or something more, a way must be found to put the life and brightness back into his old friend's eyes.

Because the Rat rested and slept more than formerly, the Mole found himself in Young Rat's company a good deal. How impressed the Mole was by the youngster's own quiet care of his "Cap'n", his unassuming modesty where his considerable River skills were concerned, and the fond way he would talk of his younger days in his "old Pa's" company.

"How long it seems that Ratty has been out of sorts. It's the first day of December already," murmured the Mole one morning, "and Christmas is almost upon us."

"Christmas?" said Young Rat. "My Pa used to mention it from his own childhood, but where we lived we never celebrated it."

"Never celebrated the Festive Season!" cried the astonished Mole.

"We were in hot climes, in strange places, where people celebrated other things at other times."

"But that's terrible. That's – !"

The Mole could not find the right words to express his dismay that Young Rat, for all his nautical skills and worldly experience, had never celebrated Christmas.

"Pa said it wasn't the same in a hot place. Said a decorated tree looked funny in the sun. Said turkey and plum pudding didn't taste the same."

Then, after due pause, he added, "Pa also said his happiest ever times were at Christmas, before he went a-wandering."

The Mole was silent awhile thinking, and then a little longer, for till that moment it had never occurred to him just how much Young Rat must still grieve for his lost father.

144

"You miss your father, do you not?" he said.

Young Rat nodded and replied, "Never had a chance to say goodbye. One moment we were together and the next the Gruesome got him and he had only strength left to get me a berth with the Royal Mail. Gave me this old marlin spike, shook my hand, and said that he'd done the best he could by me and the rest was up to me and I must make my own passage now. But – but –"

The youngster bowed his head, and the Mole, who seemed to have done a good deal of comforting of late, put his arm about him and let him sob as the River rolled by and the dank morning mist began to clear.

"Pa said – he – he –"

"What did he say?" prompted the Mole.

"He used to say he always wanted to celebrate Christmas at home just once more, but now he never will and I will never see him again."

A little time later, when a further round of sobbing was done, the Mole said, "Well! We'll just have to see that *you* celebrate Christmas this year!"

"And Mr Ratty," said Young Rat, "he can too."

"Indeed, what a good idea, what a *very* good idea – *and* Ratty too! We'll give you both a Christmas that none of us will forget and that will bring good cheer to all of us!"

The youngster brightened and his eyes lit up.

"What exactly do we have to *do* at Christmas?"

The Mole said, "Do? We don't have to *do* anything very much, except think a little of what our friends might want – for we give each of them a gift, don't you see? – and have about us only those things and people and memories that we like and cherish. Then there's the little matter of the festive board, which is to say the food and drink, in which department, if I may say so without being immodest, I am regarded locally as something of an expert. Why, my plum pudding –"

"What's plum pudding?"

"Good heavens, there *is* a lot about Christmas you don't know. For there's all the speeches and formality – that adds a little extra to the occasion, though you can take it from me that Mr Toad considers himself an authority on such matters!"

"When does it start?"

"Starts a long time back, for Christmas is in our hearts and it's always there, waiting to come forth to lighten the darkness at the turning of the winter solstice. But when does it show its cheerful face once more? Why, I think that's when the Yule log is lit in the fireplace of each and every home in the land, and those gathered there make three silent wishes, one for peace amongst us all, one for contentment to those who have had a struggle to find it in the year just past, and one for themselves, themselves alone."

Thus did the two animals talk, the Mole bringing forth memories of his happy past with which to whet the appetite of Young Rat for a better future.

"Now let us go and tell Ratty that we intend to enjoy this Christmas, whatever the circumstances! Do not mind if he complains, and says it is all too much fuss, just as he always has in the past, but take it instead as a sign he's getting better!"

But Ratty did not complain too much, and it was very soon generally agreed that this year it would be right and proper to celebrate Christmas all together.

"In which case," declared the Badger, "there is only one place to do it, and that's Toad Hall."

Toad needed no persuading, and took it as a compliment that they wished to celebrate Christmas with him.

"Of course, in the days of the old Toad Hall, and my father, when I was young," said he, "we opened our doors to all the River Bank folk, even the weasels and stoats. But in those days they knew their place and were not insubordinate. Eh, Badger?"

"In those days, I am beginning to think a great many things were a good deal better than they are now," said the Badger darkly. "I had a letter today from the Town

Hall regarding their intentions to build in the Wild Wood. We shall have to fight them to the very end! However, however . . . that is for the future. Back to more cheerful matters — let us make this a Christmas feast to remember."

"It goes without saying that we can leave the catering in the hands of Mole here, and Nephew!" cried Toad.

"Hear, hear!" cried the others, as the Mole blushed and raised his hands modestly in protest.

"My kitchen and its staff will be at your disposal," said Toad grandly.

"The invitations will be my department," said the Badger, "with Portly and Grandson to help deliver them."

"Use my letterheads, old fellow, and do not stint on the ink: I have plenty of it!" declared Toad.

"Now, when it comes to games and so forth," continued Badger, "this is an area in which Otter excels, if I remember aright, and I suggest he should be in charge!"

"Let me know what games you're lacking, Otter, and I'll send to the Town for it," said Toad.

"As for table decorations, crackers and the like," said the Badger, "I would have asked Ratty, but as he may not feel up to it at the moment, I wonder if —"

"Sir," interrupted Young Rat, "may I say something?" The Badger nodded.

"Mr Ratty would be disappointed not to do anything, so as I am his assistant, could I ask him to tell *me* what to do?"

"Now that is the Christmas spirit!" said the Badger approvingly. "I am sure that Mole will see that Ratty does not overtax himself for he is a stickler for getting things in their right and proper place."

"So am I," said Young Rat quietly.

So the day was organized, each animal having his part to play.

"But what am *I* to do, Badger?" cried Toad, who was beginning to feel that matters had rather been taken out of his control.

The truth was that the Badger remembered only too well a particular Christmas, mercifully a very long time ago, when Toad's father had most unfortunately put the matter of Christmas's organization into his errant son's hands. As a result, he had made the Badger promise that when Toad senior passed on he, Badger, would see to it that Toad was never again allowed sole responsibility for Christmas arrangements.

The Badger blinked, and a dark shadow crossed his face at the memory of the fell consequences of that dreadful hour; a day that had included an Emeritus Bishop being suspended from a chandelier, upside down; the father of the present Senior Commissioner of Police being wrapped up and given as a Christmas box to the dustmen; and – the injustice of it – the present High Judge's uncle, then the highest Law Lord in the Land, being confined for a large part of the Christmas meal in darkness in the cellars below, without even a mince pie to his name.

"*You*, Toad?" growled the Badger, forbearing to remind him of these grim events.

"Yes, me," said Toad in a small voice. "I would like to do something, if you please. It is, after all, my home. And, if I may say so, it would be reasonable if Master Toad had a part to play as well."

Badger had given considerable thought to this matter, for whilst it was wise to keep Toad well away from the organization of the Christmas festivities, they could hardly exclude him, and in any case would not wish to do so. Indeed, without Toad, disasters included, Christmas would not be the same. The Badger remembered all too well a certain party at his home that had been gloom itself till Toad had turned up and changed things altogether.

"Toad," said the Badger gravely, "I have left you till last because what I want to ask you to do —"

"Ask it!" cried Toad.

"What we all want to ask you to consider —"

"I shall do it for you all," said Toad magnanimously.

"— is difficult —"

"Nothing's too difficult for Toad of Toad Hall."

"— and demanding —"

"Demanding! Tshaw!"

"— and will take thought —"

"Thinking's my best department!"

"— and a good deal of time —"

"I have made time my servant, Badger, old fellow, and that's why I achieve so much so brilliantly."

"— and no one here could do it better."

"Well, well," said Toad, strutting about and puffing himself up. "Some lead and others follow, some can do and some can't, some, and I may say a very few and I am one, can stride the world like a giant, as the poet said, or something like it, while others merely crawl about, don't you know, and — what exactly is it you want me to do?"

"Make a speech."

"A speech?" said Toad with incredulous delight, for it was not often that the Badger offered him this concession, knowing that his speeches went on too long and generally dwelt upon a single theme, namely the glory of toads as exemplified by himself.

"We would like you to make the Christmas speech," said the Badger, "though it is a great deal to ask and you might not have time to prepare. Perhaps you would prefer it if Mole – ?"

"Mole? Ha! Can't string two words together without pausing in the middle of them."

"Or Ratty, if he's well enough?"

"Ratty? Never could make speeches except with a nautical flavour and we're a long way from the sea."

"Or myself, perhaps?"

"You, Badger? Make the Christmas speech? I don't mean to be discourteous, old chap, but you'd need a lot of coaching before you could raise a laugh from an audience, and there just isn't time."

"Humph!" said the Badger.

"Of course I shall do it! It'll take time to prepare and I regret I won't have time to help with the other things, and I'll have to find a suitable subject, and – Badger, I must go to my study at once. I'm sorry to leave you, but – My Lords, Ladies and Gentlemen – Will there be any ladies? My Lords and Gentlemen doesn't sound quite right. Will there be any Lords?"

Prattling thus, and with his time now answered for very fully till Christmas, Toad happily left them to sort out everything else.

* * *

As the Mole had hoped, it did prove to be a Christmas to remember. The heavy snow that finally began to fall three days before the festive day soon turned the countryside soft, and quiet. Yet the snow was not so thick that the field-mice, who from time immemorial had made their round of carol-singing upon Christmas Eve, could not struggle through, make themselves heard, and step shyly inside the door of each house they visited to eat mince pies and drink hot punch. Their last call was at Rat's house where Ratty was bundled up by Mole and Young Rat and put into his boat to be rowed gently up the River to Toad Hall, the choir following his passage by way of the River Bank, their lights bobbing and ducking in the dark, and the carols clear in the still and snowy night.

The next morning dawned crisp and clear as Toad's honoured guests Rat and Mole came downstairs to join Toad and his ward for the sumptuous Christmas breakfast that Toad Hall traditionally served its guests. This continued long enough for Badger, Grandson, Otter,

Portly and finally Nephew to join in as they arrived during the course of the morning.

It was then that Toad enjoined the staff to leave their own festivities backstairs to share the moment when a hall (however grand), or a house (however humble), becomes a simple home and safe retreat, as symbolized by the lighting of the Yule log.

To the Rat was accorded this great honour, in the hearth of the banqueting hall where Christmas dinner was later to be served. Happy tears came to his eyes as the fire took at the first touch of his spill, and with the birth of its flames and warmth Christmas began for one and all.

"Have you made your wishes?" asked the Mole of Young Rat.

"For peace and happiness, yes," said he.

"And for yourself?"

"I have all I want, sir; you've all been very good to me."

"There must be something you want for yourself alone," said the Mole kindly, "so wish again."

Young Rat turned back to the flames and pondered the point long and hard, and then the Mole saw him grow still as he made his wish, and he hoped it might come true.

153

"Champagne all round!" cried Toad, who on such occasions as these did not stand on ceremony and included everybody, even the bootboy.

If that meant that younger members of the staff became a little giggly, and the deputy butler a shade wobbly, and the housekeeper inclined to forget herself and kiss the butler on the cheek – and if it meant that the Badger had to sit down for a moment, and the Mole could not stop grinning, and the Otter chuckling and Portly and Nephew laughing, well, what did Toad of Toad Hall mind? His only desire was to see that all in his care were happy and content, just as they had been in his father's day, and *his* father's before that.

If, too, the staff retreated back to their own quarters full of praise for their employer, it was not because he proffered them a glass of champagne once a year, but because in that offering, and in the good and generous words he spoke in praise of them, they knew that in Mr Toad's heart, despite his eccentric and sometimes self-centred ways, Christmas was *all* the year, for his friends, for them and for Toad Hall.

Yet for one among them that day Christmas seemed a little overwhelming, and this was Young Rat, whose first it was. Try as he might to join in the games of blind-man's-buff and bobbing apples, which he had never played before, others, like Nephew, could not but notice how sombre he seemed at times, and how inclined to find a place a little apart, and stare out at the River across the snow-bound garden.

"Anything wrong?" asked Nephew, who knew that with Young Rat, as with Ratty, direct talk was best.

"I miss my Pa," said the youngster, "and wish he could see all this. The Yule log Mr Ratty lit: *he* mentioned logs. The tree with all those candles on it: he said *he* had a tree. The people, he had those about him as a lad. The games: *he* knew 'em all and more."

"Well now," murmured Nephew gently, "I think he would have been glad to see you so well set and able to enjoy all those things in his place."

"He would," said Young Rat, "but how much better if he were here as well!"

Yet Christmas would not be the same without such quieter moments of reflection and regret as these, for it is right to reflect upon the losses of the year and lay them to rest, just as it is good to celebrate the triumphs and the coming of a new season, and new hope.

"Come on," said Nephew gently, "it's time for dinner."

The great dining table had been laid the day before, though that morning it was further dusted, manicured and finished, and embellished with crackers, streamers and candles, the best silver and the mightiest serving spoons and ladles, carving knives and forks. In the centre was a great decoration of holly and ivy all tinselled gold and silver.

"I shall be making a great many speeches in the course of the next five hours or so," cried Toad once everybody had sat down but before any food was served, "and this is merely the second!"

"The third," said the Otter.

"I make it four," whispered the Mole to the Rat, who sat in the place of honour at the left hand of Toad.

"It was my father's tradition and has been my own – and one day I pray it will be that of Master Toad here as well – to propose a toast to the Uninvited Guest, whose place is always set here at my right side, though he never turns up, I'm glad to say, leaving all the more for the rest of us! Badger, you remember the old days and my father better than any of us, so would you propose that toast?"

"With great pleasure," said the Badger, rising. "For I remember my first such dinner here, in the old Hall before the fire, and Mr Toad Senior himself offering up that hallowed toast. He offered it, as I now do, in the name of those who have no place to go this day, no company to keep, no table at which to sit. People whose lives and circumstances have not brought them family or friends as we have, or have taken them far from those they love on this day when they have most need of them.

"Therefore, in Toad Hall, as in all true Christmas homes, a place is laid for the Uninvited Guest, that we think of him before we eat and drink; and reflect upon the fact that were he to come and join us, the greater blessing would be ours! And what is more . . ."

* * *

How the Yule log flamed and crackled as the Badger spoke, and how the embers glowed! How bright and cheerful the faces of those who listened to his words, nodding their heads in approval, holding their well-charged glasses ready for the toast.

Outside Toad Hall the winter wind drove the falling snow against the casement panes, to pause, swirl and settle. Along the River Bank, the old dead sedge stems trembled, the leafless willow branches swung dark against the driving sky and the River's surface flurried with the breeze, and all seemed devoid of life.

Yet there *was* one lost and lonely soul abroad.

How slowly he came, he who had no certain place to go that day! With what sinking heart he had battled for days through the snow-obstructed lanes of the country south of the Weir, sheltering beneath hedges or in a ruined barn through the long, cold nights, wondering if, come the morn, he should turn back. Yet he had not done so, driven on by hope, though he was shivering now and hungry, and as cold as bleak despair.

He who had no company to keep that day had reached the River Bank, thinking perhaps that here at last he might find respite, and a welcome of a sort, but found instead homes devoid of light and occupants. No light in the Water Rat's house where his slow steps first brought him; nor next in the Otter's, though there a hanging on the door reminded him that for some it was a happy Christmas, for some. Not knowing those parts well, and thinking he might find shelter in the Wild Wood, it was that way he turned next, and to the Badger's home he came.

"No light again!" he muttered. "And nobody at home!"

But then he saw two sets of prints leading from that old door, and though they were nigh filled up with snow he followed them, if only to give himself the forlorn sense he had company, though it had gone before.

"Hmmm!" he said, reaching the Iron Bridge. Thinking its hump almost too steep for his tired, cold legs, he pausing awhile to stare into the River. Then with a sigh and a shake of the head, he turned from the dark waters below, and began to climb.

It was then he had sight of something to cheer his eye, and lighten his heart, if only as an outsider passing by. He saw the lights of Toad Hall, warm and bright already in the darkening afternoon.

"Ah, sweet Christmas!" said he. "Those were the days!"

Then down the other side of the Bridge he walked, alongside the wall about Toad's estate, till he reached the gates, where he paused once more and stared again at the lights. Why, were those gentry folk he could see through the windows there?

"They've had a feast and a half, I'll be bound," said he, without envy or malice, "and, who knows, tomorrow, if I can find a place that will give me work along the way, maybe I'll find *my* Christmas fare."

". . . and therefore, my friends," said the Badger, concluding his toast, "I ask you now to rise and raise your glasses and join with me in a toast to the Uninvited Guest, wherever he may be, that he may find comfort and welcome this day, and bring a blessing upon the house he honours with his presence!"

They raised their glasses high, and each in his own way, but all with warmth and sincerity, uttered the words: *"To the Uninvited Guest!"*

What good spirit rose among them then and travelled out of the casement and across the snow-covered lawns, as they sipped their drink and pondered upon that person Badger had evoked? And what species of magic is it comes at Christmas, to make a mystery of simple candlelight and bring forth hope, and cause the Yule log's flame to shine with a light brighter and more far-reaching than is seen on ordinary days?

Was it then the great Friend and Helper who whispered these words on the winter wind, "Yet turn about, my friend, for seek and ye shall find"?

For as Badger, Toad and all the others made that toast, he who had travelled so very far to the River Bank, and had thought to journey on, turned back and stared again at the lights of Toad Hall, and remembered an ancient tradition he had known his father keep.

"The Uninvited Guest, dare *I* be he?"

"Yes," whispered the wind, "you may."

Toad and his guests had already sat down again and were ready to be served when there came a tentative knocking at the Hall's great front door, and the Butler looked enquiringly at Toad.

"Why, go and see who it is and if he looks half hungry invite him in, and if he doesn't, invite him in all the same!" cried Toad, for though unexpected visitors had called upon Toad Hall from time to time in Christmases past, none had ever come at this hour, at this auspicious moment, with that good toast still ringing in their ears.

All conversation and serving ceased, for there was about that knock something that stilled them all. They heard the door open, they heard quiet voices, they fancied they heard a polite protest of some kind, as of someone who had not expected to be invited in to more than the scullery, and that only for a moment or two.

Then the Butler returned and whispered in Toad's ear. Toad nodded, Toad looked surprised and then Toad said, "Are you *quite* sure?"

"That's what he said, sir."

"Then show him in!" cried Toad, leaping to his feet and flinging down his napkin. "Gentlemen, please rise and be ready to welcome the Uninvited Guest!"

Which they did with laughter and jollity, and not a little surprise and apprehension.

"This way, sir, please," they heard the Butler say. "Mr Toad really does insist on it."

"But are they not eating?"

"I rather think they are waiting for you, sir."

"For *me*?"

Then the Butler pushed open the door and ushered in the traveller.

"Mr Toad and Gentlemen," cried out the Butler formally, "I beg to announce the arrival of Mr Sea Rat, from Cairo, Egypt."

"But —"

"But surely —"

"But it can't be!"

How many "buts" there were then, though none more astonished than Ratty's, and none more dumb-founded than Young Rat's!

162

"But Pa, I thought you was dead and gone down to Davy Jones's locker!"

"I was, son, or near enough," said the Sea Rat, letting the Butler take his stick and the blue cotton handkerchief in which he portered his worldly goods. "I was –"

But explanations had to wait, for the Young Rat had sprung from his seat and across the room into his father's embrace, with tears giving way to laughter and then to chatter of delight, and finally to a faith, quite certain and for evermore, that Christmas wishes *do* come true.

The Mole, meanwhile, could not but observe – and he did not resent it one little bit, indeed it brought him happiness and hope – that the unexpected arrival of the Sea Rat had put into the Rat's eyes that look of brightness and hope that had been missing for so long, and the sense that, after all, that door upon a new world he had thought had been closed to him for evermore might yet be opened up again.

Later, after the Sea Rat had taken his place at the right hand of Toad, and several courses of their grand repast had been eaten, but with a good many more still to come, he told the story of his survival and return:

"After I caught the Gruesome, a worse pestilence than plague, and my boy was in the safe hands of the postal service, I lay down to die, at peace with the world. As I was lying there, however, I fell to thinking that I wanted to breathe the sea air one more time and since there was an Arab fellow in the market I'd done a favour for, who sold sea water fresh out of the Mediterranean for curing warts, I sent word for a jugful and I sniffed at it for comfort like, for it minded me of my old days round the Horn, and other happy days at sea.

"Well, I thought to meself I might sup a mouthful or two to remind me of when I nearly drownded in the Roaring Forties, and since it didn't taste too bad I had a bit more. Before I knew it I'd finished the jugful and was feeling a lot better!

"Bless me vitals, but in a week I was completely cured, and in a month me and my new mate, the sea-water salesman, were bottling it up as the only known cure for the Gruesome in the whole wide world, at twopence farthing a bottle!

"Afore long I had enough for my passage home, third class. Wanted to see my boy was all right and if he was, to thank Mr Ratty here for taking him in, and anybody else who's been kindly to him, which from what I've heard this hour or two past is all you good gentlemen here! So it was I made my way to the River Bank."

Of the rest of that day of celebration, memories were afterwards fuzzy and dim. Only one thing is certain: Toad made a very fine speech he had prepared upon the theme of hiking at Christmas and its benefits.

The Sea Rat, a speechifier and wordsmith to rival Toad himself, spoke at length and in detail upon the theme of good food, and his experiences in the Caliph's kitchen, which endeared him to the Mole, since it became very plain that both animals shared a common love of making food for others.

The Badger spoke wisely and well upon friendship and Christmas, so well indeed that Nephew asked that if he fell asleep again would someone kindly wake him up since he did not wish to miss too much of what the Badger said.

The Otter proposed they take a turn before dark and get some fresh air down on the River Bank, but met with no takers and instead, by general assent, they had a game of blind-man's-buff in the conservatory, followed by hide-and-seek throughout Toad Hall for the younger element.

With such pleasures the afternoon slid into evening, and the evening moved into night – and then, or some-time then, or possibly the next day, or perhaps even the day after, their Christmas celebration knew its last roundel of song and laughter, of feast and conversation, for another year at least.

Everybody agreed that there had never been a better, and from out of the winter darkness shone the light of companionship and cheer, and the hope of still better times to come.

· VIII ·
Till the First Day
of Spring

Mr Toad was so taken with the Sea Rat that at the start
of the New Year when the festivities were over and all
but the Rat had returned to their homes he suggested
the wanderer should stay with him till such time as he
felt inclined to move on.

"Mr Toad," cried the Sea Rat, "I much appreciate
your generous offer. You know me well enough by now
to see I'm not one to be anchored and battened down
long afore my feet gets itchy and my attention wanders,
so I am not likely to be a burden upon you for too long."

"But you'll stay a few weeks at least?" asked Ratty.

"I'll tell you both this and I'll tell it true: 'twas spring-time when I first left these shores more'n forty years ago and I daresay when spring sees the sap rise once more my old timbers'll be about ready for a fair sou'-easterly once more. So if your hospitality extends *that* far . . . ?"

"It does, it certainly does!" cried the contented Toad, glad to know he would have company round the place, for with the holiday over and Master Toad already back at school, Toad Hall suddenly seemed too quiet and far too dull.

"In that case I'll heartily accept," said the Sea Rat, "and make this pledge: that I'll moor myself here only till the first day of spring, and then be gone with the first watch, off to the sea once more."

"Till the first day of spring," murmured Ratty, for it was a special day in his calendar, as in the Mole's, being the day they traditionally ventured out in Ratty's boat for the first picnic of the year.

"Aye aye, shipmate, that's my pledge, for I would not wish to overstay my welcome. In any case, my son seems to have made his way here with you, Ratty, and I would not want to cramp his style and feather his sails!"

"But it means you'll be here long enough to tell us a good many more of your tales, eh Sea Rat!?" cried Ratty, his eyes alight. "You know how they thrill and inspire me so, for when I close my eyes and listen to your talk it's almost as if I'm young once more, as I was when we first met, and can half believe that I've the strength and energy to travel with you as your companion upon the seas to new places!"

167

"You've got the ebb and drift of the currents in your veins, Ratty, that's quite certain," said the Sea Rat, tucking into another of Toad's excellent buttered kippers, "just as Mr Toad here has the surge and fall of the great grand seas."

"I certainly believe I might have," said Toad, who had fancied himself of late as a sea captain, or possibly an Admiral of the Fleet, "and if I did not have family and other responsibilities to tie me down – I refer to Master Toad and Toad Hall itself – I would come with you at once, Sea Rat. Meanwhile, you were telling us last night about that clash with the tribesmen in Nisrah, when –"

"So I was, and without Young Rat at my side, and that marlin spike I gave him and which he carries about his neck, and the happy chance that we found two fit camels to make our escape across the desert, I would not be here to tell the tale!"

Many were the nights the friends were entertained thus by the Sea Rat and his tales, whether in Toad Hall or the Rat's home, and on occasion at Mole End, though this but rarely, for the Sea Rat could not abide being away from the sight and sound of the River for long.

These were good times, happy times, when the Mole allowed himself to be displaced from Ratty's company without resentment, for he now better understood his excitement at all things of Araby and the Orient, and that in matters nautical he was, himself, but a duffer, and rather in the way.

So it was with some surprise, and not a little gratification, that one evening in late February Portly brought him a note from the Rat asking if he might drop by, despite the late hour, *that we might talk alone, as in the old days – something I have missed. Please come soon, Mole old chap, and bring a bottle of your Sloe and Blackberry, for I have quite run out.*

"Of course, and right away!" cried the Mole, his face suffused with pleasure to be so asked, and Nephew glad to see that the Rat had not quite forgotten his friend.

"Mole, forgive me," said Ratty when Mole arrived with his basket, "for I've neglected you these recent weeks."

"Ratty, I understand, really I do, and I would not for one moment get in the way of your enjoyment of the Sea Rat's company, nor your dreams."

"You're a capital fellow, Mole, and I do not know what I would do without you!" cried the Rat heartily. "Now then, did you remember to bring a bottle of your best, for medicinal purposes only, of course!"

"I brought two," said the Mole, producing two bottles of his Sloe and Blackberry; "one for us to enjoy in the days ahead, and another for your cellar."

Ratty had arranged for Young Rat to stay at Toad Hall with his father for a few days, so that he and Mole might remain undisturbed, for there were many things on the Rat's mind, and he wished to have the time to talk to his oldest friend.

Then talk they did, quietly and with good humour, of so very many things, the quiet to and fro of thoughts and feelings that only friends who truly trust each other can share. Only when their talk turned to the sombre theme of growing old, and dwelt upon that subject rather too long, did the Mole cut it short.

"Why are we talking like this?" he cried, rising up and opening the window upon the chilly night, that they might have some fresh air to clear their fuddled heads. "Listen to the River, listen to the nightjar! Spring will soon be in the air again and things will be different."

But though the Rat nodded and smiled acknowledgement, he was rather less inspired by the prospect the Mole pictured. Till at last his eyes softened and, peering out of the window for a short time before pulling himself in with a shiver and closing it, he murmured, "Till the first day of spring."

"Ah, that most special of days," said the Mole, not quite sensing the Rat's uncertainty, "when we can take out your boat upon the River, and enjoy once more –"

"The Sea Rat will be leaving then," said Ratty, cutting across the Mole. "He pledged to Toad that he would do so, and has said he intends to travel south, and take a boat to Egypt once more. Just imagine, Mole: Egypt and the Nile! Araby and the Orient! Does that not inspire you?"

"Yes, Ratty, yes, of course it does," said the Mole, casting himself down before the fire once more, not sure what to say to his friend in this strange, distracted mood.

Certainly, there was no doubt in the Mole's mind that Ratty was still lacking in good spirits. Why, over the next few weeks even the Sea Rat could not seem to raise him up, nor the Badger when he came by. As for Mr Toad, his chatter and banter had finally seemed to leave Ratty more irritable than before.

By the time March came in and brought with it storms and rain and sudden chills, and a rising of the

River to dangerous levels that had the Rat and the Otter much perturbed, it seemed to the Mole that if only the Rat could be got safely to spring he would be all right once more, and all along the River Bank would see the real Ratty again.

When the River's level began to drop the Mole hoped the tide had turned in the Rat's favour. The days grew lighter, the sky brighter, and the catkins tumbled into the River in the more blustery winds.

"It's almost spring, Ratty!" the Mole would say each day. "Why the blackthorn blossom's out upon the hedgerows in the lane by Mole End! I wish you would come and see it!"

Then came a day, a happy day, when the Mole found the Rat sitting out on his porch, watching the River's flow.

"You see, spring *is* in the air!" said the Mole. "You look so much better for some fresh air!"

Yet the Mole wished it were truly so, for the fact was that the Rat looked old now, and unhappy, and as he stared at the River the old light of excitement in his eyes had gone, as it had gone in some strange way from the River as well, where once the surface had seemed to dance with reflections of sun and sky, of dawning light and fading day.

Nevertheless, after that, the Rat was always out when the Mole came by, sitting

171

and staring, standing and watching, as if trying to recapture something he had lost.

"It's almost spring, but not quite!" the Rat declared one day, adding, "And it *is* almost time for our first boat-trip of the year, eh Mole!"

How cheered the Mole was to hear him say such a thing, so much indeed that it brought tears to his eyes.

"You'll really venture out on the River then, when the weather's warmer?"

"And why not, Mole, why not?" said the Rat robustly, working as hard at raising his own spirits as at responding to Mole's. "I may have had a bad winter but I can feel the sap rising all about, and this touch of sun on my face and that blossom on the bank makes me believe I'll be fit enough to venture out, with a little help from Young Rat with launching the boat, and yourself with the oars. Why you're quite a dab hand yourself at sculling these days."

For some reason this moved the Mole greatly.

"There, there, old fellow, there's no need for tears," said the Rat gruffly. "I would just like to say that I may have been a little distant all these gloomy weeks past, but there's not been a day when I've not counted my blessings to have you aboard as a friend. You know that well enough, I daresay."

"There's no need, Ratty, really no need."

The following dawn, when the Mole awoke, he knew even before he had opened his eyes that spring was suddenly upon them. Why, there was no doubt of it, none at all, for he could scent it in the air, and hear it in the breeze, and see it in the bright colour of the sky that met his eyes when he opened his curtains.

"Nephew? Nephew! Rise and shine, for the first day of spring has come. Rise and –"

But Nephew was up and ready with two poached eggs on toast for his uncle, just as he liked them, and a pot of tea that would be brewed to perfection once the Mole had consumed the first egg and was contemplating the second, which was when he generally poured his first cup of tea.

"Will you be – ?"

"I am and we shall!" said the Mole. "Just as soon as I have made up the last few things for that luncheon-basket I have had all ready and waiting these long weeks past."

"Will Ratty be ready, do you suppose?" said Nephew.

The Mole laughed gently.

"He said to me as I left him yesterday that we should go afloat together once more, and surely today is the day!"

The Mole could resist going outside no longer and flung open the door that spring might enter their home at last.

"Just look and listen to that!"

For the birds were thronging and busy with song, and in the field the rabbits, so long dormant and only lately beginning to be active once more, were up and nibbling their way about the pasture, startled for a moment at the Mole's exclamations of delight as he stood upon his porch.

"O yes," said the Mole with touching certainty, "Ratty will have long since been up and about, working at his boat, and he'll be impatient for my arrival."

The Mole was not disappointed. He and Nephew walked down the path with the picnic gear and, sure enough, there was the Rat humming to himself on the other side of the River, working on his boat, which had been hauled up onto the bank.

"I'll leave you both to it, Uncle," said Nephew, and with that he was gone, glad to see the world was coming to rights once more.

"Ratty!" called the Mole from across the River.

"Hullo, Mole! Thought I'd see you this morning," responded the Rat, "in fact I was sure I would, for it feels to me that spring is here at last."

"Yes," said the Mole happily, sensing that something of the old Ratty had returned.

"I won't be a jiffy, old chap. Just waiting for Young Rat to come back from the Hall, where he stayed last night, so that he can give me a hand getting the boat into the water. Time was when I did it myself without difficulty, but these days . . . "

"We're all getting older, Ratty," said the Mole, sitting down upon the basket, content to wait awhile and watch the River flow by.

It was not long before Young Rat came along, and with a shove and a heave the two of them got the Rat's boat afloat. Then the youngster quickly sculled across to the Mole, securely stowed away his basket and blankets and brought him back across the River to where Ratty awaited, puffing at his pipe.

"You can take her out, Mole," he said, "and I'll be passenger, for the River's not so spry that she'll give you trouble, and I'm still a little stiff. Maybe I'll bring her back downstream later in the day."

Then Young Rat set the Mole up with the oars, settled Ratty down with a blanket about his knees and climbed nimbly ashore.

"I was nearly forgetting, Cap'n," he said before letting go of the painter, "Pa's written you this letter."

Then, having handed it to the Rat, and pushed the boat out into the water, he watched with a critical eye as the Mole struggled at the oars.

"Take it more gently, more slowly, Mr Mole, sir, and the River'll do the work for you!" he cried, just as the Rat had often done.

In no time at all the Mole had found his stroke again and even found time to wave goodbye.

The Rat was too pre-occupied with the sights and sounds and scents of being afloat again after so very long to want to read a letter just then, so he stuffed it in his pocket, saying, "It can wait till we stop for lunch."

"I hope you agree that upstream is best to start with, Ratty?" said the Mole.

The Rat nodded his agreement, for it was the way they had always gone, and any other would have been unthinkable, though the oarsman always asked.

"Best picnic spots that way," said the Mole as he set to at the oars.

"By far the best," agreed the Rat.

"It *must* be the first day of spring!" cried one rabbit on the bank to another later. "Mr Ratty's abroad in his boat, and he's got Mr Mole with him as usual."

This happy refrain was heard again and again along the River Bank all morning, as the sun slowly rose and warmed the air, bringing with it the promise of new life for beast and bird, insect and fish, glad to say farewell to the old and bitter winter that had now passed on, and give happy welcome to the new season just begun.

From time to time Mole and Ratty waved a greeting to those they passed by upon the River Bank, but for the most part they were lost in their own slow world of water and spring sunlight, of sky and shade, and of the creak of oar and plash of blade on the River's shining surface.

Sometimes they dawdled, sometimes turned; sometimes the Mole felt inclined to take them a little faster, and at others to drift back down the River for a while. But mostly they talked, or if they did not talk, then the

Rat puffed at his pipe and the Mole dreamed, and if they did none of those things they just *were*, together and companionable.

"Do you remember the first time I took you this way?" said Ratty.

"And how I made a mess of things and you had to rescue me — and you said then, as I recall, that there was nothing quite like messing about in boats and I — ignorant as I was — rather doubted you!?"

Laughter and memory filled their talk, for there was not a stretch of the River Bank they had not in some way shared together, and though the Mole had come rather later to River life, and to his abiding friendship with the Rat, they had more than made up for it in the many seasons since.

When the Rat spoke of such things to others, which was not often because that was not his way, he always said that without the Mole along to point out new things, to argue with over a point all afternoon and to share a fretful thought concerning others along the Bank, life would not have been half so rich and joyful.

Toad saw them coming along the River that day. He was stretched out in his chaise longue on his terrace at the time, thinking that if someone or other did not stand up and shout "It's spring at last!" he would, when he espied Ratty's boat and knew that they had made the declaration better than he ever could.

He hurried down to greet them and invite them ashore, but they preferred to stay where they were and talk to him while bobbing about upon the water, for they wanted to go on a little before they took their luncheon.

"At least take a bottle of champagne," suggested Toad, but the Mole declined, saying that which Toad knew well already, that champagne went to his head and, after all, he *was* in charge of the boat that day.

"Well, well, it's good to see you up and about once more, Ratty, and next time you come along I shall insist — absolutely insist! — that you moor your modest craft by my boat-house and I take you for a spin in my motor-launch."

The Rat smiled and said he certainly would when the weather was warmer, though if Toad did not mind it might be wiser if Young Rat took the helm.

"Whatever you say, Ratty!" cried the cheerful Toad. "Now, luncheon calls me too."

So they parted, the one for a dining room and a butler to serve, the others for the verdure of the River Bank, and a basket filled with all the components of a luncheon as fine in its way as any that graced a great hall's table.

"To Toad!" cried the Mole at the end of their repast, for he had not forgotten to bring a bottle of his best Sloe and Blackberry, which, though too sweet for a main course, did very well with pudding.

"To Ratty and to Mole!" cried Toad, standing at the open window of his dining room in Toad Hall. "And to the first day of spring!"

It was over lunch that the Mole reminded the Rat of the letter he had stuffed into his top pocket.

"There's a good fellow and charge my glass again while I read what Sea Rat has to say," said the Rat, tearing open the envelope. The Mole did as he was asked and noted as he replaced the Rat's glass that his friend was now frowning, sombre and still.

"Is it bad news?" enquired the Mole.

"Read it for yourself," said the Rat gruffly, handing over the letter.

Shipmate,

Spring's come round again and I must be off. I've come and seen what I wanted, and what I needed to. My son's well set, thanks to you and Mr Mole, and though the wandering life may yet appeal to him, and even take him from these shores, I'll warrant you've given him enough education in landlubbing ways for him to want to settle down and stay. I'll go knowing I leave my boy in better hands than his Pa ever had.

I will always remember our chats of ships and suchlike. It'll only take the sight of a river and the whiff of fresh water to remind me of days of happiness and comradeship I've rarely known.

I'm not much good at saying goodbye, but I'd be much obliged if you would come down to the Weir on the morrow morn, along with Mr Mole if he'll oblige me, and anybody else who cares to wave goodbye and wish me well upon my way.

I'll say my last farewell then, friend, but believe me when I say I hope all will be well with you till you reach your last mooring, and far beyond. Afore then, and knowing how you have a fancy for far-off places, I'll send you a card or two to put in that fine atlas of yours. Till tomorrow then.

Yours truly

Sea Rat

"We shall go and say goodbye, of course," said the Rat sombrely, "but I shall be sorry to do so, sorry indeed."

Mole observed that the happy light that had been in his eyes all morning seemed almost to have disappeared, and he gazed upon the River morosely now, and sadly, and in silence. The spirit of the day had quite gone out of him, and it was no good pretending otherwise.

"Ratty, there's something I wanted to say," essayed the Mole. "I mean, I – O dear!"

The Mole walked to the edge of the River and stared down into the water, which seemed suddenly dark and impenetrable, and vast, forever flowing, forever flowing south towards the sun.

"Ratty, I think I'll take a little stroll along the bank by myself, if you don't mind, just to stretch my legs before we embark once more."

"You go ahead, Mole," said the Rat quietly, head low.

The Mole trudged slowly upstream, staring at the River, then stopping to stare some more, across its surface, into the shadows of the far bank, then letting his eyes light upon a drifting twig, and from that to a sudden swirl of water, and from that – from that –

180

Why, could he not hear something beyond that swirl, beneath and about?

He sat down on the bank, as he had so often seen the Rat do, with reeds rising all about him, and the willows swaying in the breeze.

"I am sure I can hear, if I only listen hard enough," he whispered in wonder. "Help me hear, help me for Ratty's sake!"

Was that the sound of the trees behind him parting to let someone past, or just the wind? Was it the clouds that cast that benign shadow? And was it the hand of Him who is bigger than the largest tree, more ancient than the oldest rock, that touched the Mole's shoulder as gently as the River flowed?

"Listen, Mole, and hear her song. Listen now!"

The Mole obeyed His voice and listened as he had never been able to before, and heard a song that was wistful with longing, and adrift with the words of farewell, yet also full of encouragement.

"Help him, Mole, help your dear friend. It is up to you now, for my strength has all but gone and he is hardly able to hear me. Tell him what he has to do. Help him."

"I will, I will!" cried the Mole, rising suddenly, shaking his head as if to break the spell that seemed cast all about him.

"Mole! Where are you? *Mole!* Why, whatever is it?"

For the Mole came running then, running as if there was no time at all, his eyes wild, his hands and arms waving all about.

"O Ratty, you're here. Now listen —"

"Calm down, old fellow."

"No, I will not calm down, Ratty, for I am not calm, and will not be till I have said what I must. How long have you known me?"

"A very long time, Mole — a great many years."

"And have I ever given you any reason to doubt me? Or to think I cannot be trusted?"

"You have not, not once. I know nobody as sterling and trustworthy as you, except Badger, perhaps, or Otter. But I know you as the most reliable and most caring of good friends. But surely I do not need to tell you this, because —"

The Mole held up his hand to silence the Rat.

"Will you trust me now, Ratty, and not utterly reject what I am about to say without at least thinking about it for a little?"

"I suppose I must, old fellow! Whatever's on your mind?"

"Pass me the letter the Sea Rat sent you."

The Rat did so, and the Mole perused it awhile before reading out a line from it: " *'You have a fancy for far-off places.'* So the Sea Rat has written. It's true, isn't it, Ratty?"

"Yes," said he, quietly and sadly.

"Then trust me, Ratty, and follow my advice. Travel with the Sea Rat tomorrow, go *with* him, Ratty. You need the change, you need the sun, you need –"

"But I could not possibly!" expostulated the Rat, utterly dumbfounded.

"I can think of no reason why not, not one," said the Mole, turning and staring at the River, his eyes as clear as its surface suddenly seemed.

"But – !" cried the Rat, once more lost for words.

"But what?" said the Mole mildly.

"I couldn't leave the River Bank, and I couldn't leave *you*!"

Mole stared at him in silence for a time and then said, "You could, and in a way you have already. Something has broken in you, Ratty, as it has in the River you love."

"The River," breathed the Rat, going to its edge and staring at her flow.

"Ask her what she wants you to do," said the Mole; "ask her *that*! Once you nearly followed your heart and I stopped you. Now you have a second chance. Take it, dear friend, grasp it, for it will not come again."

"I am too old," murmured the Rat.

"It will make you younger."

"Mole, I am afraid!"

The Mole went to his side and put his hand upon his shoulder.

"Ask her with all your heart and she will answer you," urged the Mole, retreating quietly to pack up the picnic things. Then, while the Rat still stared at the flowing water, the Mole stowed the gear in the boat once more, hardly daring to look at his friend.

"Well, Moly," sighed the Rat at last, lighting up his briar and kicking at the bank.

"Yes, Ratty?" said poor Mole, no longer able to hide his curiosity, his excitement or his trepidation. Never had he felt more certain that something was right; never had he understood better that it was for the Rat to decide.

"Do you really think I still *could*?" asked the Rat suddenly, trying to conceal his excitement.

"I do."

"And that I would enjoy it as much as I have always thought?"

"Probably."

"And that the Sea Rat would have me aboard?"

"Certainly."

"Then I'll go, Mole, I *will* go and – why, there's no need to look quite so relieved. It's almost as if you'll be glad to see the back of me."

The Mole laughed, and perhaps cried a little too.

"It's not that at all," he said, "for I shall miss you more than words can ever say. No, it is simply that I had myself resolved, while standing upon the bank earlier, that if you did not go, *I* would!"

"Why, my dear fellow!" cried the Rat.

The Mole held up his hand.

"I do not say I want to, indeed such travel is not for the likes of me, for I am a home bird through and through. But if my going is what would have been needed for you to go, then –"

The Rat stared at his friend then, much moved.

"Mole," he said huskily, "no animal ever had a truer friend than you have been to me."

"I have often thought and said the same of you, Ratty," said the Mole simply.

The Rat let go of the painter and the boat gently drifted out into the River, to begin the homeward journey, and in a way, to begin another, greater, journey too.

As they drifted on the sun began to set, and the westward sky was filled with the warm glow of a happy day nearly accomplished, and a momentous decision having been taken, there was no need for words.

The shore seemed almost enshadowed, though the River itself was aflame with the sunset sky, and as they passed Rat's House, the Mole saw Young Rat watching quietly, and the Otter and Nephew too, and waved to them and pointed towards the Island to indicate where they were heading before they finally put back to shore.

Mole knew well enough when to stop and turn, for the Rat had often told him: "When you hear the Weir's roar, that's when to turn about. It's all very well for practised oarsmen like myself and Otter to go right round the Island, Mole, but those with less experience had best be cautious."

That roar came to the Mole's ears now, just as the Rat raised a hand to point at the Island, saying, "Look, Mole, just look at that!"

The Mole pulled in the oars a little and turned to look, and saw the sun red and gold across the sky, and the Island rising from the River, no more than a silhouette; the Island where so many years before, searching

185

for Portly and finding him safe in the arms of the Friend and Helper who watched over them all, they had together known for a time something of Beyond, and its wonder had never left them.

"O my," whispered the Mole, "it's so beautiful, Ratty, so beautiful."

Behind him, watching too, the Rat said softly, "Mole, old fellow, I never thought I would want to leave the River Bank, but now –"

"It is for the best, Ratty, and one day you'll return, I'm sure of that."

Then he turned to look at the Island once more as the Rat murmured, "I never wanted it to end, Mole, never. But you're right, one day I shall come back here and all will be well again."

"I shall be here, Ratty, and so will the River and the Island; all waiting, just as they were and ever will be."

"That's in a time beyond," whispered the Rat, "for Beyond is here as it always was and always will be, its song waiting to be heard by those of us who can hear it."

"O Ratty," whispered the Mole turning to him, and so forgetting himself in the strange and wistful magic of the moment that he let the oars drop into the water. "O my dearest friend, what contentment we have been privileged to know together here."

"Yes," whispered the Rat dreamily, "and will know together again one distant day when I return."

What cared they then that the River turned and turned the boat, for all they saw was the light that shone about the Island, and a future in Beyond that would one day embrace them both.

What cared they that the Weir's dull roar grew louder by the moment as the Island raced past? What cared they in those moments for anything, they who had touched the deepest chords of friendship two lives can find?

"Hold her fast, Portly! Let Young Rat climb aboard!"

It was the Otter's voice, commanding and assured as he and Portly swam alongside, and steadied the boat in the River's gathering race towards the Weir. While with a swift heave and final push Young Rat was aboard, to the oars in a moment, and had her back under control.

"Has Ratty been taken ill?" said the Otter, for that is how it had seemed to them from the bank.

"Not he, nor I," murmured the Mole.

"Never felt better," said the Rat.

"Then why endanger yourselves and the craft like this?"

"Well, she's in good hands now," said the Rat unabashed, as Young Rat brought her safely home.

"Never *ever* better, eh Ratty?" said Mole, laughing.

"Never," said the Rat, climbing ashore. "Now, Young Rat, it's plain for all to see that you have mastered the skills of swimming, but there's one more thing you must do before I give you your certificate as Able Seaman First Class and Distinction on the Inland Waterways, which you've earned many a time since you joined my ship, and never more so than today!"

"Aye aye, Cap'n," said the youngster with astonishment and glee.

"Look lively now and fetch your father, for he and I have matters to attend to with regard to the journey we'll be starting together tomorrow for the coast."

"Ratty!" cried the Otter in astonishment.

"Aye aye, sir!" cried Young Rat, beginning to see the import of what the Rat said.

"And another thing," continued the Rat, growing more like his old self by the minute, "take charge of portering this craft overland to below the Weir, and have her moored and ready there, the gear stowed and all ship-shape for eight bells in the morning."

"Aye aye, sir!" cried Young Rat, setting off at once to break the news to his father.

As he went off, and the Otter and Portly hauled the boat ashore, the Mole laughed with pleasure and excitement, as he had not been able to do for months past.

"Now, Mole, I'll need your help with the victualling while I get my gear ready."

"Aye aye, Cap'n Ratty, sir," said the Mole with a grin.

Then the Rat laughed too and it seemed to the Mole there was a look in his eyes as fresh and lively, as young and contented, as up and doing, as the very first moment he had met him so many years before.

·IX·
A Public Hearing

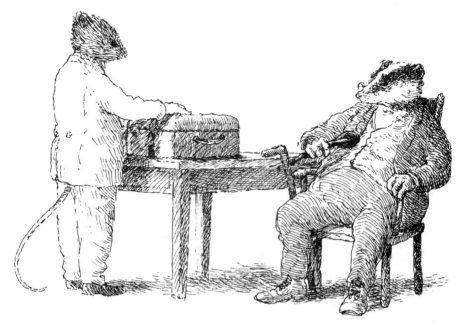

That evening, the Sea Rat having immediately declared himself in hearty approval of the Water Rat's accompanying him upon his travels to warmer climes, the news of Ratty's impending departure soon travelled along the River Bank, and brought with it a rush of excited chatter and several visits to the Rat's home.

First the Otter and Portly came by again and gave their glad approval, for they had seen at once the wisdom of the Mole's advice, and the practical good sense the Rat showed in accepting it. Then the Badger arrived, somewhat distracted and hardly able to believe his ears, though he too approved the plan, which added greatly to the Rat's confidence in the matter.

"But I trust your normal good sense will curb the Sea Rat's wilder and more unruly ideas," said the Badger, "and that you will travel slowly at first and build up your strength once more."

"I shall!" said the Rat, whose bag – for that was all he intended to take – was already packed, and whose staff – for that was the only protection he intended to carry – was by the door.

Then Toad arrived, whispering to Badger that, "all is arranged, as only Toad of Toad Hall *can* arrange such things!"

"You'll say goodbye to Master Toad for me, won't you?" said the Rat

"No need, dear chap," said Toad, "he has a special dispensation to come down to see you off, and in any case, he also has certain information that Badger needs."

"Yes, gentlemen," said Badger, "and it is information that concerns you all. My farewell to Ratty can wait till the proper time, which is tomorrow morning. Meanwhile, I am very much aware that this may be the very last opportunity we have to discuss together, in the Rat's presence, a matter that may well benefit from his advice, and one it would be remiss of me not to raise while he is still among us."

"Speak out, Badger," said the Rat, "and we will tell you what we think, just as we always have!"

"Very well: you will remember that some time ago I heard rumours that the Wild Wood is under threat of being cut down in the name of advancement to be replaced by houses. Well, it seems that the rumours are not without foundation!"

Suddenly the room was silent, as the Water Rat and his friends took in Badger's shocking news. All had hoped this matter had been forgotten.

"There is to be a hearing on the matter in the Town, next month," continued Badger. "In brief, the scheme proposes to fell the Wild Wood in two phases – the first part, further away from the River Bank but up to my own home, this year, and the second part, right down to the River Bank, next year. We will all be affected in some way – even Toad, for I understand his estate is under threat as well!"

Toad nodded unhappily.

"Two years hence, gentlemen," said Badger grimly, "there will be no Wild Wood left – unless we put a stop to this scheme!"

"We shall!" some cried.

"We must!" others declared.

"However, I am not confident of the outcome, and a significant portion of those affected, namely the weasels and many of the stoats, support the scheme –"

"Shame! Down with the rascals!"

"Gentlemen, please!" cried the Badger. "The weasels have represented to me their very strong belief that new accommodation for their brothers in the Town, where they now live in crowded slums, should be provided here – though I believe the stoats are divided on the issue.

"I can only remind you how important it is that those who have views on the matter, whatever they may be, should express them forcibly in writing – nothing less will do – to the personage whose address I shall give you in a moment, and you should also be willing to attend the Public Hearing in Town upon the twelfth day of May."

"We shall!"

"We must!"

"Surely," cried the Otter, "if enough of us are against it they won't proceed, will they?"

"I fear that they will, Otter. This is not a matter of democracy but of money and influence, and while my Grandson here has been diligent locally trying to gather information about who is behind this scheme, Master Toad – ah, I think I hear him coming at last, so he can tell you for himself!"

There was a loud roaring outside, which came to a sudden stop. The door opened and in came Master Toad, in all the protective gear of a motor-cyclist, for such pursuit he had recently taken up.

After a good deal of further chatter and talk, and a quick display of his new motor-cycling skills, which were still so raw that he very nearly landed up in the River, Master Toad accepted a cooling drink and, prompted by the Badger, told them all that he knew.

Master Toad seemed to have grown up a good deal in recent months, and though he had not yet acquired that comfortable, plumpish build which was so much part of Mr Toad's persona, he was well on the way to it.

"*Mes amis*," he began, his initial nervousness betrayed by this lapse into his mother tongue, for he was not yet as used as Toad to public speaking, "I shall not waste words but what I 'ave to say is confirmed by what Grandson has learnt from the workmen who 'ave been marking out where the trees will be guillotined down and 'ouses built.

"Three people 'ave formed what you call a consortium, a group, and have bought the Wild Wood and the canal and a lot more. They do not 'ave the River, that's the Monarch's, nor the land on the other side, because the Village owns that —"

"Who are the three rogues who want to cut down the Wild Wood?" asked Nephew.

Master Toad paused for effect and said quietly, "They are friends of my pater."

"But, Toad, surely you can make them see sense," said the Mole. "Wherever did you meet these vagabonds?"

"In court," said Toad in a subdued voice, "which is just it, don't you see? The three scoundrels Master Toad refers to are the Most Senior Bishop (whom he and I once insulted) and the Commissioner of Police (from whom he and I once went on the run) and the Very High Judge (before whom he and I have appeared in a variety of ways, though very few of them to our advantage)."

"And these are our enemies?" said the Mole.

194

"The three most powerful personages in the land after the Monarch," said Master Toad.

"So our cause is hopeless?" said Nephew.

The Badger hesitated, and glanced at Toad as if the two knew a little more than they were letting on.

"We may not be able to stop this destruction to the River Bank," he said finally, "but that is not the same as saying there is no way out. There is hope of a kind, but not much. We must attend the Hearing and decide what to do when we learn the outcome. But I would not have been comfortable in this enterprise if Ratty here had not heard this news, bad though it is, and given us the benefit of any thoughts he has on the subject."

"My thoughts are plain and simple," said the Rat without demur. "However hopeless the case may seem we must protest and if necessary fight! We must never give up. I shall not be here to fight at your side, much though I would wish it, but Mole will speak for me, should the need arise, and if it helps, let him join my name to those of every other protester! We must not give in till the last, and then –"

"And then, Ratty?" said the Otter. "What then?"

"Then, my friend, be practical. Do not waste time on a lost cause. Turn your minds to other ways of going forward, however hard they may be, however impossible they seem. That's something Mole here taught me long ago – and I shall carry it with me on my journey, as I hope you will bear it in mind in the months ahead. More I cannot say."

But it was enough, quite enough, to give a harder edge to the purpose the Badger had shown them, and the sense that though the Rat himself might not be with them, his spirit would always be at their side.

Thus did the Rat's last evening among them end, and they all dispersed, promising to be up and ready the following morning to see their friend off upon his travels.

Dawn came bright and early, and full of the hustle and bustle of new life, of new arrivals – and new departures.

"It was on a day such as this that we first met," declared the Rat as he and the Mole, accompanied by the Sea Rat and the others, with the exception of the party from Toad Hall who had yet to arrive, set off for the far side of the Weir, "and it is fitting we have another such morning on which to make our farewells."

"How I shall miss you!" cried the Mole, who felt excitement for the Rat and sadness for himself in equal measure.

"I shall be back, Mole, in good time; and you did say, did you not, that you would wait for me?"

"I *did*, Ratty, and I shall, always! But write to me occasionally and let me know you're well and have seen at last those places whose names you know only from the atlas and the Sea Rat's tales."

"My atlas!" cried the Rat, stopping suddenly. "I quite forgot to say that I wanted you to have it, or rather to keep it safely for me till I return. I shall write as often as I can, and perhaps you will mark within its pages my passage through Araby and the Orient?"

"I shall, Ratty, I shall!"

The Mole and the Rat chattered on, and Sea Rat and his son said their own farewells, with many more kind words from Badger and Grandson, till the company reached Ratty's boat, now heavily laden with the victuals they might need for the voyage to the coast.

Toad arrived soon afterwards, and made a rousing speech, declaring that the Rat was a capital fellow and that in journeying from the River Bank he carried all their hopes with him. Toad might have said a good deal more had his speech not been drowned out by the arrival of the Village band, whose members had taken dangerous and precarious stations upon a traction engine, especially hired and driven for the occasion by Master Toad.

Then amidst hissings of steam, the blaring of wind instruments, the huzzahs and farewells of all their friends, the Rat and the Sea Rat finally embarked, and with an expert push from Young Rat, were suddenly off and away.

"Goodbye," they all cried.

"Goodbye, Sea Rat!"

"Farewell, Pa!"

"Goodbye, Ratty!"

Till only one still cried farewell from the Bank, alone yet not lonely, wistful yet not sad, and that was the Mole.

"Goodbye, dear Ratty!" he called out last of all, as Master Toad tooted the whistle of the traction engine and set off to accompany the travellers as far as the Weir road would allow him. "Good luck, my friend!"

Then, at the last, as the boat reached a turn in the River beyond which it would not be seen, the Water Rat gave the oars to the Sea Rat for a moment and turned, and waved his final farewell to the Mole.

Yet one last voice had still to join itself to theirs. For the sun was rising with the day, spring was all about, and there rose in the air the River's voice, content now to see her most faithful of companions off and away upon his travels, off for a time beyond her ken.

The Mole heard her song, and understood its words.

"She sings not of farewell," he murmured, wiping away a tear, "but of the safe return of one who could never have found final contentment here till he had journeyed afar. Ratty will be back, he *will!*"

Then all came and stood by the Mole, and watched till there was no more to see.

In the weeks that followed Ratty's departure the Mole had no time to grow sad, even had he wished to, for there was much to do in preparation for the Public Hearing concerning the future of the Wild Wood.

No one was more vociferous in their support of the Badger's opposition to the scheme than the Mole and Mr Toad, yet when it finally came to the attendance at the Hearing in May, they suffered the indignity of being turned away at the doors.

It seemed that the good folk of Lathbury, and in particular the customers of the notorious Hat and Boot Tavern, were on the march, intending to fan the flames of the Wild Wood dispute and so gain publicity for their own cause, which was the right to free access to

Lathbury Chase, the great fell above their village which had been in the High Judge's family since the eighteenth century.

Anticipating trouble, the Town Authority had posted a platoon of police constables by the door of the Town Meeting Hall in which the Hearing was to take place, as well as eight formidable mounted policemen. This array of helmets and blue uniforms brought out a cold sweat upon Toad's brow, for he and constables did not get on well, and trouble usually ensued when they met.

It transpired that only those individuals who had received a Notice of the Hearing and had brought it along (a copy would not do) were to be admitted – which fortunately included the Badger. Unfortunately, those who were unable to produce such documents were not to be admitted, and that included Toad, the Mole and Master Toad.

"But I'm Toad of Toad Hall, Constable!" cried Toad, considerably put out.

"That may be so, sir, or it may not be, it is not my part to say," replied the Chief Constable affably, "I am merely here to uphold the laws of the land, under which, namely and pursuant to the Residential Public Hearings Act of 1907, Section 63, paragraph 5 –"

"O, bother all that," said Toad. "I'm affected, so let me in. Indeed, there was a conference of residents along the River Bank last month which I may say went so far as to take a vote upon the subject of my participation in, and speaking at, the Hearing today, very much as Members of Parliament are elected by their constituents and . . . "

Toad paused at this point, fearing perhaps that the Chief Constable might enquire more closely into that non-existent vote, but instead the officer allowed a firm and resolute expression to settle upon his face as he said in measured tones, "None shall be admitted without the proper authority, sir."

"Pooh!" cried Toad, making a sudden and foolish dash for the entrance, and signalling the Mole and Master Toad to do likewise.

The Mole was glad he chose not to follow Toad's advice, as several large officers descended upon the two toads, while all further advance was blocked by two of the mounted policemen and the Very Chief Constable was summoned.

"I wouldn't advise you to do that again, if I were you, sir," said he to Toad and his ward, both by then suspended by the scruff of their necks by burly constables, "for we would not want to place you under arrest. If my memory serves, sir, you have seen the inside of the Town Gaol before, have you not, and are a known trouble-maker?"

The constables unceremoniously deposited the considerably chastened Toad and Master Toad some way from the Meeting Hall door, along with their accomplice the Mole, at the feet of the various onlookers who had gathered there to enjoy the fun.

"It isn't fair!" said Toad, brushing himself down.

"No it isn't!" declared Master Toad less good-humouredly. "Not to admit a citizen of the land, and then when 'e protests to threaten 'im with gaol. In France that constable's 'ead would not stay long on 'is shoulders if the citizens 'ad their way!"

Just lately Master Toad, in whose final year at school the study of European history had loomed large, had been studying the French Revolution and had discovered some radical roots he did not know he had.

Master Toad's sentiments might well have inflamed the passions of a Parisian mob, but in the Town passions rise more slowly and the best one member of the crowd could do was to shout, "No, it ain't fair, but what do you expect when the Very Senior Bishop himself is involved? Not fairness, that's for sure!"

"And the Commissioner of Police!" cried the indefatigable Master Toad. "That gentleman is in on it too!"

"Is he?" asked another.

"That's a scandal!" declared a third.

"And what's more," cried Toad himself, seeing that the crowd was gathering about him and unable to resist the opportunity it offered, "the High Judge is lining his pockets too at the expense of us Wild Wooders!"

"That's right, and he's inside the Hall right now, conducting the meeting hisself in his own favour!" thundered another protester.

"Won't be for long, not if the men of the Hat and Boot get their way!"

"What's that?" called out Toad, for he had fond memories of the Hat and Boot Tavern in Lathbury, a low dive from the clutches of whose angry customers Ratty and Mole had once rescued him.

"You don't think the Wild Wood's the only scheme his High Judgeship has got his fingers into, do you, mate?" said Toad's latest ally, quickly informing Toad of the matter of Lathbury Chase.

"It isn't fair!" cried Master Toad, sensing this to be the best slogan for the day.

"No," cried Toad, "it isn't fair!"

"Please, Toad," begged Mole, for he could see that the crowd might soon turn ugly, "I really think it would be wisest if we left this matter for Badger to debate inside."

"Pooh, Mole!" cried Toad, the gleam of public glory in his eye. "Debate and discussion never achieved anything. It isn't fair!"

"No, I suppose it isn't fair," began the Mole.

But these were unwise words to repeat, for hearing them and thinking he was one of the leaders, the crowd hoisted the Mole upon its shoulders along with Toad and Master Toad as the chant grew loud and rhythmic, and police and protesters swayed back and forth.

"It isn't fair, it isn't fair, Toad of Toad Hall says it isn't fair!"

Meanwhile, inside the Hall, and with the three personages so heavily involved in the scheme all present on the platform (one presiding, one watching out for breaches of the peace, and one praying), Badger was coming to the end of a long and well-argued speech against the scheme.

"We have natural right and justice on our side, m'lud, and the rights of commoners as well, and thus far we have been peaceful in our protest, and I may say very reason —"

The chanting from outside was louder now, and almost sufficient to drown the Badger's measured words.

"— reasonable, I say, and peacef—"

There were sounds of skirmishing and the neighing of horses and shouting of men.

"– peaceful, as I have suggested and –"

Then outside it was suddenly peaceful no more.

Hoisted up as they had been, Toad, Master Toad and finally even the Mole, rather let things go to their heads and shouted all the more, playing to the growing crowd around them, who were loving it.

Even so, the constables might have contained the mob had not a formidable army of men, women and children, not to mention some very rough-looking weasels and stoats, just then appeared from that cobbled way that is called Lathbury Turn.

Toad saw them, and knew them at once, for many of them were Hat and Boot customers.

Perhaps, after all, he did feel a momentary pang of terror and fear, and saw visions of the interior of the Castle's deepest dungeons, and its condemned cell, which he knew so well, but such inner warnings did not survive long.

No longer, indeed, than the first cry of the Lathbury folk upon seeing him.

"It's Mr Toad come to lead us!" they cried. "And 'e's got his own set of followers to help and the constables are trying to arrest them! Come on, lads!"

This analysis of the situation was not quite accurate, but as Toad himself had said, what *is* the use of discussion and debate?

The Lathbury men joined in the fray, someone put an umbrella in Toad's hand as an emblem of his authority, and he waved it and uttered his battle cry, "It isn't fair! Charge!"

So unseemly a mêlée as then ensued had not been

known in the Town's long history since the notorious St Scholastica's Day riots of 1355 when the common folk were similarly put upon by those who held power and authority.

In very short order the constables guarding the entrance to the Meeting Hall were displaced, and three of the mounted policemen rapidly dispossessed of their horses, and Toad, Master Toad and the reluctant Mole put in their saddles instead. The other mounted policemen immediately attempted to put right this gross indignity by chasing after the miscreants all about the Town, which led to other horses bolting, vegetable carts being overturned and shop windows being broken.

Worse still, the old familiar madness quite overtook Mr Toad, who foolishly stole a policeman's helmet and put it on, while Master Toad, not to be outdone it seemed, rode up the Cathedral steps and uttered words which if not quite blasphemies, certainly lacked the grace of good divinity.

As for poor Mole, a less able horseman than these two, he was left suspended from the ladder rest of a street light, whence he was rescued and promptly arrested by a posse of constables.

A great deal was said in the Magistrate's Court the following morning: of how the Public Hearing had broken up in disarray, the Very Senior Bishop temporarily de-frocked, the Police

Commissioner handcuffed back to back with the Chief Constable, and the Very High Judge summarily tried and found wanting by the unruly Lathbury Mob.

There *were* mitigating circumstances, however, the most substantial of which was the extraordinary horsemanship and skill displayed by Toad, the policeman's helmet now firmly stuck on his head and quite obscuring his view, who as chance and good fortune would have it, galloped back through the crowd so that the High Judge was able to grasp the reins of his horse and so be dragged off to safety even as he was about to be strung up on a hastily erected gibbet in the marketplace.

"All in all," said the High Judge in his summing-up, his bruises still showing, "I am inclined to take a lenient view of those unseemly proceedings, if only because your leader, Mr Toad, showed himself at the last moment to be contrite and sensible and to put the upholding of life and liberty of the law before all else!

"A month in gaol for the lot of you, and a fine of ten shillings each to you leaders, Mr Toad, Master Toad and Mr Mole, and Mr Badger. I will only add this to you, Mr Mole and Mr Badger, who have not been in my court before and whom I had understood to be upright and sober citizens. Do not commit another crime within my jurisdiction or your fine will be much larger, and your custodial sentence eternal!"

"Yes, m'lud," said the chastened Mole.

"I won't!" growled the Badger.

"Case dismissed!"

"Another triumph!" crowed Toad as they went below to begin their sentence, for he had readied himself for the death sentence and felt that a month in gaol (with time off for good behaviour) at someone else's expense was not so bad considering what fun they had all had.

"Triumph?" growled the Badger as the doors of his cell were opened to admit him. "We went to protest against the felling of the Wild Wood, not to be put in gaol for a month! I greatly fear that the Town Authority will take advantage of our enforced absence from the River Bank to cut down the whole of the Wild Wood! This is not a triumph, Toad, but the beginning of the end of all we have known and loved!"

· X ·
Farewell to the Wild Wood

The Badger was not far wrong in his predictions,
though the Wild Wood was still standing, and in the full
glory of its summer colours, by the time the four of
them returned to the River Bank.

Waiting for each of them this time, however, was
formal Notice of a second Hearing with special dispensation for only the Badger and the Mole to attend,
which in the Badger's view was a wise proceeding.

But of that infamous Second Hearing, upon whose
outcome the lives and happiness of so many depended,

the Badger did not afterwards care to dwell. Naturally he and the Mole attended it, but the popular voice was made mute by procedure and fine print, and numbers were much down on the earlier Hearing, owing to various farmers and other landowners affected having been made certain offers they found it imprudent to refuse.

After a desultory debate, in which bewigged lawyers were more in evidence than ordinary people, the matter was decided in favour of the original proposals, with a few changes to accommodate the needs of those who had dropped their opposition and accepted whatever offers they had been made.

With respect to the Wild Wood the opposition of existing residents, principally the Badger and a few diehard weasels and stoats, was discounted in favour of the many it was deemed would benefit, and it was decided to proceed with the destruction of the Wild Wood "within thirty days".

It was also decided that with respect to the Toad Hall estate, Toad should be instructed that if he did not stop obstructing the scheme and sell his land and the Hall as well for development he would be held in contempt of the Court of Common Council – an ancient court over which, as it happened, the presiding officials were the High Judge, the Commissioner of Police and the Very Senior Bishop – and arraigned before it.

Only one part of the River Bank remained safe, and that was the part on the east side occupied by the fields surrounding that sunny, happy nook popularly known as Mole End. This remained within the jurisdiction of the Village, whose council, realizing the danger, had arranged for Mr Mole, and the rabbits who lived in the fields thereabouts, to claim squatters' rights, and gave them all Deeds of Ownership and Protection to prove it.

The Badger and the Mole came back from the Town despondent and down-hearted, for there now seemed little they could do. In their absence Toad had been visited by various personages, some mere functionaries and others more important, some acting on behalf of the three eminent gentlemen who stood to gain so much from the scheme, yet all with much the same message: sell your land, accept our offer of extra compensation, or it will be worse for you in the end!

Reporting this to his companions, Toad sighed and said, "I say to them and say again till I am tired of it that I shall do nothing, absolutely nothing, without the agreement of my good friends along the River Bank, and even then only if certain conditions are met."

"You are very good about this, Toad," said the Badger, "but you must not —"

"My dear fellow," said Toad, "my only regret is that my father did not buy up the Wild Wood when he was offered it, for a song I believe, a good many decades ago, and then we might have been in a position to put up a better fight."

"Even then —"

"Even then, Badger, I cannot help noticing that the offers of compensation that these gentlemen keep making are steadily increasing and are now rather more than double in value than when they began. If my informant, namely Master Toad, who knows the sons of those three rascally personages rather well since he is at

211

school with them – what a sensible Toad I was to send him where the education was so to the point! – if he is correct, their offers will go up a good deal more before they come down. Have a glass of champagne, Badger, and you too, Mole, for I can afford it and you look as if you need it!"

"But Toad," protested the Mole, "you know very well that it does not agree with me."

"Pooh, Mole! You always say the same. It agrees with you rather too well I think."

"But –"

"And you, Badger, you'll have one too, for in different ways we all need to drown our sorrows."

"Do you know, Toad," said the Badger, "I think I shall!" He suddenly felt a good deal more heartened than he had for many months past, for the whole affair had been a very great strain and had begun to affect his health and well-being. Now that it was settled, albeit against his wishes and interests, that wise animal saw that he could at least get on with other things, and begin to ponder the future.

They sat then, those three, and talked as they had not been able to since the Rat's departure, and while the Badger and the Mole said a good deal more than they were wont to, Toad said a good deal less. He seemed content to listen for once, content to sit with those who through the years had always been there, and though they might disapprove of what he had sometimes done, and the way he had done it, yet never once, not for a moment, made him feel that he was not always welcome in their homes and, he almost felt inclined to add, in their hearts.

Perhaps they felt better able to talk because the young-sters were not there, though the youngsters (as they still called them, though that term now seemed increasingly inappropriate) were very much on their minds.

Toad suddenly sighed, stood up and went to one of the large windows of the conservatory and gazed across his garden down to the River. Then after a moment or two he exclaimed: "You know – I do believe – I think – I say, you fellows, there *might* be a way!"

"A way to what?" enquired the Badger, puzzled by Toad's sudden animation.

"A way to get out of this mess we find ourselves in," cried Toad. "Mind you, it is not my idea but Master Toad's, and when he first mentioned it I was rather dismissive. But now that the Wild Wood is certain to be chopped down, I begin to see that he might have been right after all. Yes – *yes!*"

He turned to them, hopping about from one foot to another, his face excited in a way it had not been for years, though it cannot be said that the Badger and the

Mole looked anything other than dubious. Toad's schemes so often ended in disaster.

"I know what you fellows are thinking," said Toad good-humouredly, "but hear me out, and if you can think of a better way for us all to get out of this pickle, I shall be glad to hear it.

"You see, Master Toad has made many useful contacts in the Town, and he is of the opinion that once the Wild Wood is destroyed Toad Hall and its estate will not be worth living in, with all those weasels and stoats taking up bijoux residences so nearby. His view is that it would be best to sell it to the highest bidder and – and here's the thing – buy some place as yet unspoilt, and this time buy enough of it that it never *can* be spoilt!"

"But where would there be such a place to buy?" said the Badger. "And, though it is not quite my business, would you have the wherewithal to buy it?"

"The offers I have received for Toad Hall and its land are very considerable," said Toad, "and might perhaps provide us with enough –"

The Badger's eyes softened, for irritating though Toad could be, his generosity of spirit and his largesse where others were concerned had never been in doubt. Here he was allying himself with them both, and with the River Bank, and seeking a way forward for all of them, not just himself.

"In any case," said Toad, "I have a fancy to have a new hall built upon virgin land, that I might stretch my wings and have a little more space about me!"

The Badger laughed heartily that Toad should claim to feel cramped in his vast home.

"I told Master Toad that I did not approve of his scheme but of course he ignored me and said he would have his contacts look about for an estate to exchange for this. I shall let him know that I have changed my mind. It was thus that my own father taught me to be radical and bold, and so must I encourage and educate my ward!"

The Badger nodded most approvingly, and though the idea was but vague, and hope of it ever being viable and being brought to a successful conclusion unlikely to be fulfilled, yet he had to admit he saw no other way.

A few days later all such hopes and dreams quite fled their minds. The inhabitants of the River Bank seemed scarcely to have drawn breath upon the dawn, and opened their curtains to see what prospect the day had in store for them, before the grim and terrible sound of traction engines was heard coming from the Town Road. Not long afterwards a good many were seen coming over the Iron Bridge, and very soon the sawing of wood was heard and the first tree was felled.

The Badger was too late to see this proceeding, so swiftly did the destroyers act, but he was there to see other trees fall, and within but a few days a great swath had been cut through what had taken decades and centuries, millennia perhaps, to grow and form, change and mutate, a swath that cut right into the heart of the ancient and awesome Wild Wood.

Thus far the Badger had seemed to cope well with the threat of change that had hung so heavily over them all, and perhaps those contingency plans that he, Mole and Toad had discussed had given him heart. But now, with the foresters daily cutting down more trees, and builders digging footings for the new homes, the strain began to take its toll.

As the destruction of the Wild Wood inexorably progressed, and day by day its sounds grew nearer to his own home, and the bigger trees that had dominated the skyline of the Wood disappeared, he grew morose and angry. No doubt Grandson bore the brunt of this, though he never said so in so many words – but his friends would find him from time to time standing by the River, angry and upset and complaining that the Badger's mood was becoming too much for him.

The Mole saw that there might be more to it than that and so, remembering Badger's kindnesses and good advice to him so often in the past, he decided to visit the Badger on a day when he knew Grandson was off with Nephew.

He knocked on the Badger's door, and heard at last that animal's approach, and the gruff, "Who's there?" As he waited he couldn't help thinking how torn and ragged the Wood had become. Its darkness had all but gone, and clear sky shone through the remaining trees, whence came the roar and whine of machines, and the rude shouts of workmen and foresters.

"It's me! Mole!" he called in response to the Badger's second wary shout.

The Badger's door opened and out he came, spectacles upon his nose, still in his dressing-gown, his hair unkempt.

"Look what they've done, Mole! Look what they've done to the Wild Wood!"

The Badger did not bother to change his dressing-gown for something more appropriate, nor did he even shut his front door, as he had been wont to do – for this had always been a dangerous place to live and an animal was wise to leave his bolt-hole secure.

"There's no one here now but me, Mole," he said bleakly. "All my neighbours have gone, and the weasels and stoats have fled to temporary accommodation till their new homes are built and they can come back. Here, let me take you on a walk you will never, *must* never, forget!"

For days afterwards the Mole could not rid his mind of the sadness and grief in the Badger's eyes as they had walked together through that desolated landscape.

"The critics of the Wild Wood have said its trees are ancient and unproductive," Badger had said, "and many are dangerous because branches keep falling down. Well, of course they do, Mole, that is the way with woods and forests. An oak branch tumbles, a birch tree falls, and in their place, where light comes down, new life grows. That fast-growing birch they have felled over there would have given protection to this tiny oak you see they have trodden on. That oak branch cracked and fell that others upon the same trunk might have a chance. It was always thus, Mole, from the beginning of time. We old ones must give way to the new. But not like this! Not *this*!"

Old trees and young, all were cut down, uprooted and pushed aside that the men and machines might get to the next. All ruined now, the more pathetic for the semblance of life that showed itself in the green leaves of the fallen branches, though on the smaller of these the leaves were already drying and curling for lack of nourishment, as if autumn had come six months too soon.

Where proud trees had fallen many of the bigger branches had cracked and broken, whether from crushing under their own weight above them, or from the strains and stresses of the fall. This wood was white and shining still with sap, good wood now dying, great trees now fallen.

The Badger had no words to express the loss he felt for a place he had known all his life, and whose changes had ever been subtle and slow, whose life was every bit as important to him as his own.

"We along the River Bank have always revered the River before all else," said the Badger, "but the River and the land it flows through, which includes the Wild Wood as well, are one, all one."

There was nothing the Mole could say, nor could he imagine a worse agony for the Badger, whose front door now opened onto rack and ruin.

The Badger was right: that was a day the Mole would never forget, even if he tried to, as long as he lived.

Yet something was still to happen that was more cruel, something more undermining of Badger's strength, and it was all the harder to accept or understand for being so unexpected.

Suddenly, the felling stopped, and the machines fell silent. No men came that day, nor the next, nor the next after that. It was as if a terrible storm had come upon the Wood, torn its very heart out, and then moved on, leaving behind destruction, and no explanation.

A week went by, and then another, and still the men did not reappear, nor the destruction resume. The Badger sent a letter to the Town to enquire what was happening, and then another when no reply came; and then a third, to which a brief and quite unsatisfactory answer was all that he received.

July came, and amidst the uprooted trunks of trees, hewn saplings and torn earth that had been the Wild Wood, new life began to grow. The leaves of brambles, their root stock still intact, began to unfurl, and show themselves to a world they thought they had lost forever. Rose-bay willowherb began to rise, and even to flower pink-red, where formerly they never flowered at all; while foxgloves, normally sickly in those parts, were now able to begin to rise from the ruins all about.

The Mole walked with the Badger one hot summer's day amongst this strange mixture of lost life and new hope, and he saw that the Badger had aged badly. He stooped now, and seemed to hear far less well, for which affliction he had taken to carrying an ear trumpet, though this did not stop him mumbling to himself.

"Badger? Badger!" he was forced to shout.

"Eh, Mole? Eh?"

"Have you heard anything more from the Town about what they propose to do?"

"They've stopped, that's plain, and the Wood's – the Wild Wood's – beginning to – beginning again –"

He turned almost full circle, looking about as he struggled to make himself say "beginning to recover again" but could not. The Wood could not recover in his lifetime. For him the true Wild Wood was gone forever, however much the brambles, the fire-weed and the foxgloves might hurry to catch up on growth they had never expected to make.

That sadly memorable walk, despite the new life so much in evidence, made the Mole even more despondent than the first, for he saw now that the Badger had begun to give up, and to withdraw.

"Badger?"

But the Badger turned and picked his slow and unsteady way back towards his home, not hearing the Mole's voice, or perhaps not wishing to.

A few days after this, with August almost upon them, they heard some scandalous and shocking news from Master Toad, who had recently left school and taken up a well-remunerated position in the Town's financial district: the gentleman who had been paying the foresters and builders had gone bankrupt and his creditors were to take him to court. The work had stopped because there was no more money and none could say if, or when, it might be resumed.

"But it won't be the High Judge, or the Senior Bishop, or the Commissioner of Police who suffer, it seems," growled the Badger, putting down his newspaper, "for they are in the clear, as their kind usually are. They will simply find another contractor to finish off the work."

His fears were soon fulfilled, for a week or two later the traction-engines were back, the work began anew, and all that little re-growth in the Wood laid to waste once more.

It was in this hour of new despair, when Grandson reported a further decline in the Badger's health, that the Mole ventured to the Badger's home once more in a state of high excitement.

"You're to come to Toad Hall at once, Badger, *at once*. Today Toad received the highest offer he thinks he is likely to receive for Toad Hall and all his estate!"

"I trust he accepted it," grunted the Badger, thinking this was not news to get excited over.

"That's just it, he *didn't*, or rather not yet, for at the same time Master Toad has discovered that there is a property for sale that might suit Toad's scheme of moving away. So, he's gone rushing off in his launch, with the Otter at the helm, and says he may not be in time but —"

"But what, Mole?" said the Badger.

"It was your son Brock who alerted him, and Master Toad who confirmed it by telegraphic communication. You remember that land I saw from his home when I first met Grandson, that great domain —"

"The place you called Beyond —"

"It will always be Beyond to *me*," murmured the Mole, with a distant gleam in his eye.

"– that far-off wild place which you thought that one day Nephew and Grandson, and others of the younger generation might seek to explore?"

"Exactly," said the Mole coming back to earth. "Well, it seems that it is known as Lathbury Forest and that a part of it might be for sale. Toad has gone off to buy it, and if he does, well –"

"How much is for sale?" said the Badger.

"Just a bit, I expect," said the Mole, "yet enough for our humble needs."

"When is Toad due back?"

"Today, tomorrow, you cannot quite tell with Toad."

"Not today, I think, a night at the Hat and Boot will be too tempting for that animal. But tomorrow, Mole, despite my present weakness, and even if it is the last thing I do, we will call upon Mr Toad and, if we need to, knock some sense into his head. Our original plan was one thing, but it sounds like folly to give up Toad Hall and all its ground for a scrap of fell and forest land that will be no use to man or beast."

The Badger was as good as his word, and the two were ready and waiting in Toad's conservatory when he returned jauntily next day in time for lunch.

"Up and about again, eh Badger? And you, Mole?"

He paused, and a hunted look came over him.

"I fear you have come to admonish me?" said he, for he had seen the Badger, and others, look this way at him before.

"Why, what have you done?" said the Badger.

223

"Done? Not much," said Toad, pulling a worn and folded piece of parchment from his pocket. "Well, something of which I daresay you will disapprove. It will mean I will have to vacate Toad Hall within the month, and you will have to leave the Wild Wood, that I guaranteed. But Mole will still have Mole End and we can all stay with him!"

The Mole looked uneasy, but Toad only laughed.

"Have you sold Toad Hall?" said the Badger.

"I haven't sold it exactly," said Toad, "because the agent of the Church Commissioners, who made the best offer on Toad Hall, finally agreed to a swap."

"A *swap?*" said the Badger. "For what?"

"Er, well," said Toad hesitantly, "I didn't actually *see* what it was for because there was a lot of mist about –"

"You exchanged your inheritance for a parcel of land sight unseen!" exclaimed Badger.

"That's the lingo, Badger, that's what the Very Senior Bishop said: 'parcel of land' and 'sight unseen'. Just so."

"The Bishop?"

"Signatory for the Church Commissioners who was there with the agent, and if you ask me, which you won't, they didn't seem to know a great deal about property dealing, whereas I and my partner –"

"Your partner?"

"Master Toad was there too, but had to rush back to the Town this morning to arrange the exchange and agree the completion. Wanted to do it fast lest the mist cleared and they changed their minds. These youngsters, they seem to do everything so quickly now: rush, rush, rush. As I was saying, Master Toad has studied

property and portfolios and that sort of thing, and said we should –"

"Should what?"

"Exchange Toad Hall and all its land for this little bit of paper –"

The Mole and the Badger were aghast.

"– which is only a copy of a small part of those deeds that will be mine, or rather *ours*. Well, I could not leave you out, Badger, seeing as you will soon have no home, or any of the River-Bankers, old or young –"

"And these other deeds, supposing they exist, are for what exactly?" pressed the Badger.

Toad started to read from the paper: "'Excepting that parcel of land which Mr Toad, late of Toad Hall, or kin and beneficiaries . . . ' – that's Master Toad; he told me to put it in – 'may choose for themselves, but not to exceed half the whole estate, the River-Bankers (whose names are herein attached) shall hereby have conveyed unto them that piece or parcel of land, or those pieces and parcels of land which abut that wilderness known as Lathbury Pool, that fell known as Lathbury Chase, that . . . ' and it goes on a good bit more in that vein, Badger, till we get to the bit that Master Toad says is what matters.

"'' . . . and which is commonly called, and has been since the beginning of recorded time, as mentioned in the Domesday Book itself, by the name and title "Lathbury Forest".' There! That's about it!"

"But, Toad, you exchanged Toad Hall for a few trees sight unseen just because there was mist in the way?" cried the Badger, rising from his chair in consternation.

"Whether there was mist in the way matters not one bit," said Toad, "because it would not be very easy to see all of it from one place even if the day was crystal clear!"

"Why ever not? How large is it?"

"About two hundred and fifty thousand acres, I believe," said Toad nonchalantly, "which makes it the largest estate in all the land, excepting the larger of the Monarch's estates. All very good hiking country I'm told. Only trouble is there's no right of access."

"No right of access?" thundered the Badger.

"Forgive me for interrupting," said the Mole timidly, for Toad and the Badger appeared now to be ranged against each other, "but what might 'No right of access' mean?"

"It means," said the Badger in a hollow voice, his eyes wild, "that Toad has exchanged Toad Hall for a rude and rugged wilderness to which he cannot go because to do so would mean crossing someone else's land, for which he will need a permission he is presumably never likely to get."

"O my!" said the Mole.

"Did you bother to find out who owns the land upon which you cannot go without trespassing?" asked the Badger dismissively.

"Of course I did," said Toad, utterly unperturbed. "It is owned by the High Judge –"

"The High Judge!" cried the Badger now in complete despair, for if there was one person in the land least likely to grant Mr Toad, formerly of Toad Hall, right of access, it was that representative of justice who had done battle with Toad so many times in the past, and had so often found him guilty and wanting.

"But, Toad," cried the Badger rising wildly, "how could you *possibly* have committed such folly?"

"Fear not, Badger, for I have a plan."

"Another plan!" cried the Badger dismissively. "It had better be a good one."

"O it is, very good, and it is just as well. You see, last night I spent a good deal of time in the Hat and Boot at the invitation and expense of the men of Lathbury, among whom I am something of a hero."

"And?"

"And that worthy group of gentlemen, recognizing in me a leader born and bred, and one who is not only selfless on other people's behalf, but also fearless where injustice is concerned, have asked me to lead them in a mass trespass of Lathbury Chase, that same land that prevents me getting to my new estates."

The Badger and the Mole stared at Toad in amazement, caught between grave doubts about his idea and excitement at the sheer boldness of his plan. As they did so, Toad strutted about, seeking to look like a leader born and bred, and there was in the Mole's eyes a return of that old admiration for an animal who always saw a way forward out of difficulty. It seemed a very long time since he had been in such a scrape as this, and frankly the Mole felt excited at the prospect.

"I'm with you, Toad," he cried, "and I know Ratty would be were he here!"

The Badger was more circumspect, frowning and pacing about while Toad winked at the Mole as if to say "You see, he'll come round."

"Unless," said Toad at last in his most winning and disarming way, "you can see a better way for us all to get out of the mess we're in?"

The Badger came to a stop and said, "I cannot, not at all. And I suppose – old though I am, and portly though *you* now are, Toad, and a touch greyer and more lined though our friend Mole here is these days – I suppose that if we *are* to say farewell to the Wild Wood, and the River Bank as well – for farewell it will surely be – then Ratty would have been the first to have agreed that we might as well go out fighting!"

"Hurrah!" cried the Mole as Toad danced about and clapped his hands, making cuts and thrusts in the air with an imaginary sword.

"Meanwhile," said Badger, "before we set off upon this new enterprise, I trust I have time to say my last farewell to the Wild Wood?"

The Badger *did* have time, for it took nearly a month for Master Toad to conclude matters on behalf of his pater, and Lathbury Forest to be put into Toad's name – subject only to completion of the sale of Toad Hall and all its estate to the High Judge and his partners.

During that time, the Badger saw the last trees felled, and those ancient tunnels and secret places he and his father before him had delved beneath the Wild Wood, briefly exposed by the bulldozers before they were covered up again and flattened in preparation for building. But by then his grief was all done and, moving for those last days with Grandson into Toad Hall, that wise animal sought to put all behind him, and think only of what might yet be, if Toad's new scheme found success.

He found support from an unexpected quarter – the Otter. That sterling animal had long since decided it was time to leave the River Bank, but had been reluctant to say so, for he had rightly feared that the Badger might take the news hard. Yet with matters turning out as they had, and the Badger with new possibilities in mind, the Otter broke the news.

"Often talked with Ratty about travelling south down the River to the coast, you know," said he.

"No, I didn't know," said the Badger; "but now Ratty's gone you've thought of it again?"

The Otter nodded with resignation.

"The River's not the same without him, but she wanted him to go. Now I feel the same, Badger, and Young Rat's keen to come with me. Portly's old enough to look after himself now, I think – indeed, he'll be better off without me. But I'd like to explore the River

229

below the Weir, and Young Rat will need companionship for a while before he decides if he's to follow in his
father's footsteps and travel abroad once more, or come
back to stay amongst you in your new home."

"You're a sensible animal, Otter, and always were,"
said the Badger. Then he added wisely, "As for Young
Rat, he needs to see the world a little more before he
settles down otherwise he'll be restless all his life. He
could not have a better companion than you to help
him make up his mind about his future."

A few days later the Otter and Young Rat slipped off
down-river, and the River Bank seemed suddenly even
more empty.

For Mole and Mole End, his home for so many years,
matters were less brutal than they had been for the
Badger, though no less distressing. Try as he might to
clear out the contents of his little home and put them

into storage till a new home might be found, he could not do it, and he packed and unpacked three times at least.

Finally, one of the rabbits who lived nearby, who had always been on the best of terms with him and held him in high esteem, agreed at Nephew's suggestion to hold Mole End's keys and look after the place "till Mr Mole returns or decides what he wants done with his house and effects".

This formula gave the Mole the comfort of being able to believe that Mole End might stay the same, and that one day – well, they would just have to see. This much agreed, the Mole took his final leave of the beloved place on the morning of Toad's planned departure, in his launch, for Lathbury, and the adventure of the mass trespass.

"Goodbye, Mr Mole! Goodbye!" cried the rabbits as he left in a carter's dray, with only his much-loved luncheon-basket, his cudgel and one or two other such precious items to hand.

"Goodbye!" said the Mole, turning and waving, his face wet with tears. "Goodbye!"

He looked back at his home one last time and then resolutely turned back, and looked back no more.

"Drive on!" he called. "Drive on."

In later years, if Nephew ever had to choose the moment when he knew his uncle to be as courageous a mole as ever lived, it was that moment: when, growing old, his face grey and lined, most of his life left behind him in Mole End, Mole was still young enough in heart and mind to move on from the past, and look forward with interest and excitement to the future, however uncertain it might be.

· XI ·
Toad's Finest Hour

Toad's final departure from Toad Hall was accompanied by a great deal of pomp and circumstance, much to the embarrassment of the Mole and the Badger, who would have preferred to leave the River Bank quietly.

To make the occasion more enjoyable Toad hired a band to put on a display of music and marching on his lawn, concluding with a rendition of "Hail the Conquering Hero Comes" as, after many a tearful farewell, he climbed aboard his launch accompanied by his friends and left Toad Hall for the last time.

As they travelled up the River they knew so well to join the Lathbury men for their mass trespass, they

acknowledged the cheering crowds on the banks and
Toad's chest swelled ever larger as he looked forward to
the glorious battle that confronted them. When his
magnificent flotilla of craft came at last to the outskirts
of Lathbury, however, our hero's face fell somewhat, and
a look that suggested a cowardly desire to escape the
scene suddenly came upon it.

The cause of this change was very plain to see as
they neared the stone bridge that stood adjacent to
Lathbury's notorious Hat and Boot Tavern, the agreed
rendezvous for the start of the trespass.

On the Lathbury bank of the River, all the town's
menfolk had assembled, along with many of their wives,
mothers, sisters and a good many of their children. On
catching sight of Toad's launch, with its master standing
seemingly so brave at the helm, this group let out a great
cheer and the men raised their staves and cudgels.

Toad had no sooner seen this display of raw and
warlike intent, and realized with considerable alarm that
this was not to be the quiet protest he had imagined,
than he heard an answering shout from the other bank,
where a number of the High Judge's gamekeepers,
wardens, grooms and other estate workers were standing.

A good few of these large, tough-looking gentlemen
carried staves as well, and the gamekeepers had twelve-
bore shotguns. Plainly they meant business, and they
answered the Lathbury folk's welcoming shout with a
roar of disapproval and contempt.

Toad saw that he was as much the target of this verbal
assault as he was the focus of the cheers and hopes of the
Lathbury side. As they approached the Hat and Boot

Tavern, with rival forces gathering on either side, what fuelled his alarm still more was the sight of the massed ranks of constabulary upon the bridge, there to keep the peace.

The faces and eyes of these stolid and well-armed constables had about them a fierce and determined look, and caught as they were between two opposing factions, their mutual gaze fixed itself upon Mr Toad as if he alone was the cause of the trouble.

There was no way back. However much he might have liked to turn about and flee, the crush of supporting craft upon the River, not to mention the presence of police boats, made this impossible. Instead Toad found his launch heading gently for the bank by the bridge. Immediately several sturdy officers, including Toad's old friend the Senior Commissioner of Police, hurried down the bank, grasped the painter of Toad's launch, and hauled its unhappy and now frightened admiral ashore towards a pair of waiting handcuffs.

The Commissioner of Police was very well aware, however, that arresting Toad in full view of the rebellious mob that for some peculiar reason so revered him might prove unwise.

"Mr Toad," essayed the Commissioner, raising his voice somewhat because the crowds were becoming increasingly raucous, "I wish this affair to end soon and peaceably and you would be ill-advised to provoke the forces of law and order further. I therefore offer you this chance of speaking to your followers. Please urge them to go back to their homes without causing an affray!"

Toad was only too happy to accept this offer, thinking he might slip away unseen, but the Lathbury men immediately jumped to the conclusion that he was being arrested, and surged forward, and as the constables attempted to restrain them, tempers became even more frayed.

Worse still, the moment Toad realized that so great and powerful a personage as the Commissioner himself was not only encouraging him to make a speech, but had actually ordered the constables to aid his passage to the most prominent part of the bridge and raise him up that he might be heard, his earlier fears fled him and he felt suddenly dangerously light-headed. Toad liked nothing better than an audience, and now the cries of encouragement and support from the Lathbury men so swelled him up with vanity and pride, that all common sense left him at once and he felt impelled to speak out.

"O, please be sensible, Toad!" cried the Mole, who by now had clambered out of the launch with the others. "Please do not say anything too provocative!"

"Provocative?" cried Toad, waving his arms about and climbing up onto the bridge's balustrade that he might be seen by his audiences all the better. "I shall *certainly* be provocative!"

The Lathbury men cheered at these wise and noble words, while the constables looked on helplessly, for Toad was rather beyond their easy reach and they were in danger of pushing him into the River if they tried to stop him speaking, thereby provoking a full-scale riot.

"For what common and ordinary citizen of our noble realm would not be provoked at the sight of such bullies and thugs as we seem to see upon the far bank of the River?" continued Toad in a loud voice.

This initial sally from Toad brought complete silence,

as all waited to see if he would continue in this vein. But Toad, so full of pride a moment before, now saw the angry faces of the High Judge's men, who seemed so much bigger and stronger all of a sudden, and decided there and then that he must immediately retract, recant and escape. Perhaps with a quick a leap into the River and a hasty swim downstream, he might yet escape with his life.

Then there came a shout from the Lathbury side that puffed up his pride once more, making him quite forget the danger.

"You're a great gennelman, Mr Toad, and we're glad you're going to tell those brutes the truth!"

This ill-judged remark came from Old Tom, Toad's old drinking companion from the Hat and Boot Tavern, and it provoked a good many cheers and huzzahs of the kind Toad found even more intoxicating than the Tavern's ale.

"Brutes they certainly are!" cried Toad to renewed loud cheering, though he needed no further encouragement. "Brutes in mind and body, who think nothing of threatening the honest citizens of Lathbury with their sticks and guns!"

"Mr Toad," called out the Commissioner, who now saw that his attempt to win Toad's support had gone horribly wrong. "I am hereby placing you under –"

"Listen to the voice of corruption!" called out the very foolish Toad, who intended to enjoy himself while he might. "Listen to the man who seeks to protect with his corrupt constables those who have purloined the common land!"

The cheers at this, and accompanying cries of right-
eous anger (on one side) and rage (on the other), were
loud indeed, and both sides so pressed and surged
forward upon the bridge that the outstretched arms of
the arresting officers were swept harmlessly away from
where Toad stood.

"But, my friends," continued Toad ecstatically, "their
truncheons shall not hurt us, for liberty knows no pain,
and their handcuffs shall not stop us, for freedom knows
no restraint!"

"Liberty!" "Freedom!" "Deliverance!" The cries
came thick and fast now, answered by an ugly roar from
the other side.

Toad threw caution to the winds and continued more
boldly still: "The guns of the coward, I say, shall not
frighten us! For the great tree of freedom cannot be
felled, nor can death itself take from us our dream of the
land of liberty —"

"Hurrah for Mr Toad!"

This last cry, though somewhat less raucous than the
others, was still loud enough to be heard by most, and
rather surprisingly it came from the Mole. He had been
so carried away by his friend's eloquence that he too had
lost all sense of public order and propriety.

This sudden display of support from one whom all
knew to be a law-abiding citizen was too much for the
Senior Commissioner. Having signally failed to arrest
Toad when he should have done, and then compounded
the error by letting that dangerous and criminal animal
incite his followers, the Commissioner decided that an
example might as well be made of the Mole – and

Nephew, Badger, Grandson and Master Toad too.

Now Toad might very well be a coward and fool unto himself from time to time, but he could not abide injustice, especially not threats to ones he held as dear as his River Bank friends. They could arrest *him* if they must, but his friends they must leave untouched.

He turned to point past the angry ranks of the High Judge's men up towards Lathbury Chase, whose purple heather was gloriously ablaze with autumn sunshine, a beacon of liberty and hope if ever there was one.

"See there!" he cried. "They wish to rob my brave friend Mr Mole of that sight of freedom forever, as if it were not enough that they have exiled him from his lifelong home at Mole End! They seek as well to cast their shackles upon Mole's brave young Nephew and Badger's Grandson, that they might grow old in the confines of a dungeon in the Town Castle!"

"Shame on the constables!"

"Destroy the gamekeepers!"

"Throw the lot of 'em into the River!"

Toad raised a hand to quieten the mob, as assured in his command of the situation as any Roman orator. Indeed, if ever there was a moment in Toad's long and eventful life when he actually resembled the imperial and triumphant Toad depicted by his cousin Madame Florentine d'Albert-Chapelle in the statue she had made for him some years before, which still stood in the grounds of Toad Hall, this was it.

A baying rabble. A raised hand and imperious stare at friend and foe alike. A decline towards silence and an expectant hush. And Toad, speaking once more.

"What is more, they intend to flog my young ward Master Toad, light of my life, hope of my dotage, and lock him up in a solitary confinement that his sensitive soul and fine feelings will not long endure – and as for Mr Badger, whom you all know to be a wise and honest gentleman, I understand they already have the rack and hot irons ready for him that he might make a false confession!"

It was enough, and if Toad said more his words were never heard. He had said enough to inspire the men of Lathbury to action and they now began to break the police ranks and throw as many as they could into the River below, while their wives and children hurled after the defeated constables anything they could lay their hands on, pots and pans, brooms and brushes, shoes, butter churns and cobblestones and a good many empty beer bottles, supplied by the new landlady of the Hat and Boot, who had been trying to clear out her cellars for some months past.

With the constables pushed aside and scattered, and the briefly arrested Mole and the others swiftly freed, the mob reached the top of the bridge. There Toad had time only to gasp, "Now, steady on, you fellows, I really think perhaps we ought − to − think − again −" before he found himself hoisted from his vantage point, and placed upon the broad and sturdy shoulders of the Lathbury men.

From this new, unstable and moving vantage point Toad discovered he had fallen prisoner to his own eloquence. Cry out as he might, struggle though he tried, Toad could not break free from the eager hands that held him, nor escape the brutal and savage charge down the other side of the bridge towards the High Judge's waiting men, of which he was the reluctant figurehead, leader and vanguard.

"No − really − I mean − perhaps we could − *help!*"

It was all in vain that Toad looked round desperately for aid from his friends, for they too had now been hoisted high upon massing human steeds far beyond the control of any one of them.

It was a challenge, a danger, to which they each responded differently. The Mole, who was renowned along the River Bank for the way in which once moved to ire he could fight alongside the best of them, was no disappointment now. He had his trusty cudgel in his hands and as he was borne swiftly down towards the High Judge's men he swung it about 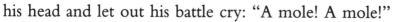 his head and let out his battle cry: "A mole! A mole!"

Nephew, normally as little given to anger and assault as his uncle, was now inspired to grasp one of the milk churns and set upon the enemy with gusto, ably supported by Grandson.

Master Toad, who had come dressed and armed like a cavalier, had fortunately had his rapier struck out of his grasp early in the fight. He was reduced now to flailing about with his fists, which since his arms were short and he had been hoisted high was more impressive than effective.

The Badger, too frail to do more than allow himself to be carried about as if he were the regiment's colours, was nevertheless too high off the ground to get seriously hurt, and began to quite enjoy himself.

Whilst Toad, the very first to reach the front line of the High Judge's men, and therefore the first to receive their insults and blows, had decided that as with speechifying so with battling, and he began belabouring all about him with a garden hoe supplied by his supporters.

Of the historic battle that now ensued no two accounts agree, nor can ever agree, since everything became utterly confused. There was no doubt, however, that Toad was finally felled by a blow to the head by a gamekeeper soon after the ranks of the High Judge's men were broken and the charge began up the fell towards the top of Lathbury Chase.

He lay semi-conscious and forgotten among the heather and peat-hags for most of the action, only vaguely aware of the angry cries about him.

He did not see how the police re-grouped upon the bridge and set off in pursuit of their aggressors, nor how the High Judge himself, having most sensibly deployed only half his force at the bridge, had stationed the rest of his men at the top of the fell, where they lay waiting out of sight.

So it was that, filled with the first flush of success, the now leaderless Lathbury men broke ranks and ran up towards their objective without a thought, right into the ambush so cunningly laid by the High Judge, and were there beaten, defeated and turned back.

Of all this Toad knew nothing, nor that the battle was all but lost even as he woke up to a throbbing head, and the scent of heather and of peat about him. He sat up gingerly, appraised the gravity of the situation and fell back into the heather with a sigh.

"They will come and arrest me now for sure," he told himself, "and I shall be returned to the Town Gaol from where I shall never come out alive. O despair!"

Toad stared up at the sky and began to feel very strange indeed. It was true that his head ached, but he did not care; and that all his limbs hurt, yet it mattered not. Yes, he felt most peculiar and he began to reflect upon the fact that never, ever in his life had he done anything so glorious as make that speech.

So many to listen to him. So many to follow him. And yet it had all been but words, just words and vanity and conceit, as the Badger had always said.

Toad lay pondering these things for some time, and might very well have remained there till the constables found him, had he not heard a terrible groaning nearby.

He sat up once more and what he saw made him forget all his own aches and pains, and put from him all selfish thoughts and vainglory. For there was poor Mole, a crude bandage about his head, and Nephew tending him, himself cut and bleeding from the fray, while not far off Grandson was carefully applying a bandage to Badger's arm.

"Toad, tend to Mole," grunted Grandson, "while I look after my grandfather."

"Dear Mole," whispered Toad, who felt both chastened and angry as he went to his old friend and knelt at his side.

The Mole opened his eyes at Toad's voice and said, "Did we really lose the battle, Toad?"

"Well, Mole, I don't think we can claim to have won it," said Toad quietly, seeing the Lathbury folk dragging themselves back towards the bridge, and possible custody.

"So we did not find the freedom of which you spoke," whispered the Mole. "We did not reach the land of liberty."

"Freedom?" repeated Toad. "Liberty? Well, I did speak of those things, and I meant what I said, but – but –"

The strangeness that Toad had felt earlier now returned to him, yet more powerfully, seeming like a singing in his ears, a distancing of all about him. Slowly Toad sat up. He felt again the troubling aches and pains in his limbs, and felt too a tightening about his chest, and it frightened him. As did the line of men that stood guard over Lathbury Chase: six gamekeepers, a few constables, a great many grooms, and the Commissioner of Police.

"Mole?" said Toad softly. "Might I borrow your cudgel for a time?"

The Mole sat up a little, much surprised at this request.

"Of course you can, Toad, but what – ?"

Toad picked up the weapon, and he looked at Nephew with a brief smile, perhaps even a modest rueful smile, which in its simplicity and ruefulness was quite unlike any that had ever been seen upon the face of Toad of Toad Hall before.

He pulled himself up to his fullest height and said, "You know, Mole, old fellow, it *isn't* fair."

"What isn't?" said the puzzled Mole.

"This," said Toad, pointing at the ranks of the establishment forces, and at the trailing army of the defeated, "it just isn't fair! Freedom *can* be found and the land of liberty *may* be reached! And were our old friend Ratty here he would not give up. Mole, we must go on!"

Toad had made a good many speeches in his time, but he had never said anything so powerful and direct as those words he spoke to the Mole upon the battlefield.

"But, Toad!" cried the alarmed Mole. "Where are you going? You can't – you mustn't – O my! Wait for me!"

How small and vulnerable those two now looked as, with Toad supporting the Mole – or perhaps each supporting the other, they began their slow progress towards the land of liberty. Neither looked back, and so they did not see the stirring hope that came now to Nephew's eyes, nor the admiration and awe that came to Master Toad's. They did not see how the Badger nodded to Grandson, and knew that after so many years, Toad was finally reformed.

"We must not let them down!" cried Nephew.

"Nor shall we!" declared Master Toad. "Here, Nephew, I have an idea. If you've strength enough, hoist me on your shoulders, for unless we muster support –"

Nephew understood the point immediately, and without further ado knelt on the ground so that Master Toad could climb upon his shoulders. It was a struggle but with Grandson's help, Nephew managed to stand up once more.

"I say, you fellows!" began Master Toad.

"Louder!" cried Nephew.

"You over there!" he tried again.

"Louder still," gasped Nephew, for Master Toad seemed to be getting heavier by the moment.

Then Toad's ward let out a great rallying cry and as all heads turned in his direction he pointed to Toad and Mole.

"It's Mr Toad!" he cried. "*He's* not defeated. And Mr Mole as well. *He's* going on. Turn about and follow them! Support them! Help them in their battle against the landlords and the –"

Poor Nephew could sustain Master Toad's weight no longer, and tottering first to one side and then to another finally toppled them both forward into a grubby peat hag before the rallying speech was finished.

But Master Toad had done just enough. The Lathbury men nearest them turned to where he pointed, saw Mr Toad and Mr Mole, and cried to others near, "Look! The fight's not over yet! Mr Toad's pressing on once more!"

This astonishing news spread swiftly amongst the retreating Lathbury folk, and they saw that it was true: their hero Mr Toad was not defeated, and if that was so, and one as small and vulnerable as kindly Mr Mole was following him, then *they* must rally and lend their support as well.

They turned back and followed Mr Toad once more, whilst the High Judge's tired men, some already sitting in the heather from fatigue and premature jubilation at their victory, saw to their astonishment and horror that the foe were regrouping about that rabble-rouser Mr Toad, and were coming up in numbers even greater than before. For the Lathbury men had been joined now by the wives and youths who had come out in expectation only of helping their injured, and by children who till then had stayed well clear of the fray.

Not only were the waiting guardians of the Chase now clearly outnumbered, but all hope of reinforcement was gone, for many of the constables had drifted down towards the bridge, and others of the High Judge's men had done likewise, lured by the prospect of free ale.

Sensing their foe's unease, the Lathbury men hurried to catch up with their hero Toad, who, resolute still, was marching ever nearer the waiting ranks of the enemy, with poor Mole trying to keep up with him and Nephew and Master Toad now but a short way behind.

It was when they were but a hundred yards from the enemy, that the glorious view of the higher and more distant hills and mountains to the north came in sight.

The Mole's gaze shifted from the threat ahead, and focused on the more distant prospect, whose half-hidden vales and slopes, and steep cliffs and rises, were bathed now in an autumn evening haze, golden red, and beautiful.

"Toad!" he whispered incredulously. "That vision you see there is Beyond. It is the place that Ratty and I tried to reach all those years ago, but of course we never could."

"Beyond?" said Toad, astonished. "That is no such thing. That is Lathbury Forest, which we now own, and which is to be our new home, if only we can gain a right of access to it this day!"

"But –" said the Mole.

"No buts, Mole, the enemy's only just ahead!"

Then, even as the nearest of the High Judge's men raised a stave to strike him down, Toad turned to the Lathbury men and, pointing at the summit of the Chase, commanded his followers: "Take it in the name of freedom!"

Then Toad fell, though whether from a blow or from his own fatigue even those closest to him could not say. The hand that had pointed in the direction of victory now clutched at his chest, as he cried out: "Follow them, Mole, defeat them, do it in memory of the River Bank! Do it for Toad who was once of Toad Hall!"

Without hesitation the Mole took up his cudgel and,

waving it about his head, bravely led the last charge of all, with Nephew and Master Toad and Grandson close by and the Lathbury men all about, till the High Judge's men broke ranks and fled, and the battle was won.

A short while later, when the first flush of victory was over and the crowds upon the Chase had cheered and sung, and admired the view to Lathbury Forest so long denied them, Master Toad said suddenly, "But where's Pater? Where is he?"

When he saw that Toad still lay where he had fallen, he ran back, followed by Nephew and Grandson, and finally, when he could break free of the admiring crowd, the Mole as well. Not long after the Badger came up to join them.

The red warm light of the setting sun was upon Toad's face and he seemed peaceful and content as he lay with his eyes open, staring not at the celebrations upon Lathbury Chase, but towards the more distant prospect of Lathbury Forest.

He looked at the Mole and then at the others, and then back towards his new domain, and said, "Is victory ours?"

"It is Toad! O, it is!" cried the Mole. "And all thanks to you!"

"Sadly, I shall not be able to enjoy its fruits," said Toad, sighing a good deal, and shifting about as if to ease the aches and pains of his warrior wounds.

"Why is that, Pater?" asked Master Toad.

"Because I am near death," said Toad. "But at least I shall pass on in the knowledge —"

"O, Pater!" cried Master Toad, weeping effusively. "Please do not die!"

"Really, Toad, I do not think –" began the Mole, but the Badger raised his hand.

"Let Master Toad handle this," he whispered, "for I do believe he has the measure of Toad better than all of us. His tears are surely no more convincing than Toad's sighs and groans."

"Do not weep, Master Toad, or mourn for me," continued Toad stoically, "for my life is fulfilled in this action today and I – I – aaah –"

Toad writhed about a good deal more, and then closed his eyes and put his head more heavily still upon his ward's chest as if trying to summon up strength for one last attempt at coherent speech before he finally left them behind forever. As Toad's eyes closed, however, his ward's expression changed from abject sorrow to simple enquiry.

"Mr Mole," said he in a low voice, that Toad might not quite hear, "where is that victory 'amper you prepared this morning?"

"Why, it's in Toad's launch," said the Mole, "but is it quite appropriate if Toad is so weak?"

"Nephew, fetch it, will you?" commanded the Badger, beginning to understand Master Toad's drift.

While Nephew hurried off, the rumour spread that Mr Toad was mortally wounded, and soon crowds flocked towards where he lay – so much so that Grandson had to hold them back.

"O, let them nearer, pray," said Toad in a frail and faltering voice, raising himself up a little to hear rather better the common folk's wails and lamentations at his imminent demise.

On Nephew's speedy return Master Toad asked, "Mole, is there perhaps some *champagne* in your basket?"

"There is," said the Mole, still hesitant.

"A Moët and Chandon?"

"It is the one that Toad has always most preferred," said the Mole.

"Then open it, please, Mole, and pour a glass for my pater, and for all of us."

At this Toad's hand tightened upon that of his ward, and his eyes seemed to smile and express pleasure, anticipation and contentment, and he sat up a little straighter.

The champagne was poured, and a glass was placed in Toad's other hand.

"Pater, you always said that at such a moment as this you would like a glass of champagne in one hand –"

"– and a good Havana in the other," murmured the

ever thoughtful Mole, taking out a box of them, for he had often heard the same.

Toad smiled, and seemed to recover a little, for he nodded and said, "Yes."

Then, letting go Master Toad's hand, he took the cigar that the Mole proffered and sniffed it appreciatively, and sat up without support.

He put it to his mouth, at which the Mole lit a match for him. He sat then quietly, a glass of champagne in one hand, a Havana in the other, the one merely sipped, the other merely puffed at once or twice.

"Do not leave us, Mr Toad, surr!" cried Old Tom from among the crowd. "Do not desert us till that dastardly Judge concedes defeat!"

"I shall not!" said Toad, raising his glass to them.

It was just then that the proceedings were interrupted by the sudden sound of the High Judge's voice – something not at all well received by the Lathbury folk. Why, that man had caused so much trouble, and his men had brutally beaten Mr Toad to the ground. Now he seemed bent upon disturbing their hero's peace even in his dying hour!

Toad saw at once how matters lay, and how ugly they might quickly become. He waved a welcoming hand, he managed a smile, he seemed to wish to say that he could not quite get up but – but –

"Give him a glass of champagne," said Toad at last, and it is doubtful if words of reconciliation and forgiveness could be better or more succinctly spoken.

The High Judge took the glass with good grace, and he raised it to Mr Toad, and in a brief speech declared that he did not wish to disturb Mr Toad or his friends any longer than he must, but wished it to be known that in view of the events of that day, in view of all he had seen and much regretted seeing, he had been persuaded to oppose the common people no longer and had even now given instruction that this fell, and all others over which he had rights or influence would henceforth be of free and unfettered access at all times to the public, bar perhaps a few days once in a while for grouse shooting.

Better still, he declared that he would convey to Mr Toad a parcel of land that would ensure access to him, his friends and his inheritors now and for evermore from the highway that ended at Lathbury right up into Lathbury Forest. In short he yielded to all the demands that the Lathbury folk and Mr Toad had made.

His speech was followed by great cheering, and several of the Lathbury men lifted the High Judge onto their shoulders and, as Toad raised a glass in cheerful acknowledgement of the High Judge's graceful and immediate surrender of his rights, he indicated to Master Toad that he might just like to be raised up himself for a moment or two.

This brought a further cheer from the crowd, members of which, led by Old Tom, came forward and gently raised the hero up onto their shoulders. From this new eminence he raised his glass in the direction of the High Judge, and proposed in a voice still heroically weak that their differences all be forgotten, and since the afternoon was advancing rapidly and the air growing cold, that the meeting adjourn to somewhere more comfortable.

Then it was that Mr Toad, formerly of Toad Hall and now owner of the Lathbury Forest estate — whose value had been trebled that day as a result of the access gained — and his neighbour and good friend (for now he surely was) the most important legal personage in the land, were carried off the fell in triumph for something more robust than champagne at the public bar of the Hat and Boot Tavern.

· XII ·
Return to Mole End

In the months that followed, Toad, Mole and Badger led the younger generation in quiet colonization of Lathbury Forest. The best site was chosen, with a river nearby which might well be regarded as the River itself had once been before the noxious influence of the expanding Town had begun to spoil it, for its waters flowed full and wide, and were clear and pure.

It cannot be said that the Badger was ever as active again as he had been in the great days of the River Bank. Yet on all matters his advice was often sought, if he could be persuaded to emerge from the comfortable quarters that Toad had built for him in a part of the Forest near the finest stretch of the new River.

As for Toad, he was not long without spacious and stylish accommodation, for on hearing that the medieval palace of a former Chancellor of the Exchequer was about to be demolished on the far edge of the Town, to make way for a shoe factory, he had it removed stone by stone and set up anew not far from where the Badger had chosen to live.

Here the daily needs of these two old friends were met by a willing staff whose employment and organization were seen to by Master Toad's agents – he himself being far too busy with matters in the city, where he was rapidly increasing Toad's wealth and estate, to spend much time in the Forest himself.

As the months passed into years, the Badger grew more reclusive still, and he and Toad ever more inclined to talk than do; to dream than take risks; to laze in Toad's comfortable chairs and chaises longues and enjoy their memories of a happy and exciting past, and contemplate a future they no longer felt they need worry about too much.

Then, one winter, quietly, with his old River Bank friends and all his family about him, the wise old Badger died, at peace with himself and the world. He was buried in Lathbury Churchyard, where Toad and the Mole each spoke a

257

moving funeral oration to his memory. Having cast soil in the traditional manner upon the coffin, the Mole and Grandson cast something else in the turf and soil all about: which were seeds, and many of them, of the trees of the Wild Wood, which Grandson had saved in the hope that one day, in a better age perhaps, the Wild Wood might rise again.

Through those same years, as Nephew and Grandson, and Master Toad too, though at more distance, willingly pressed/ on with their purpose of creating life anew in Lathbury Forest, the evening of Mole's life grew ever more quiet and contented.

He was content to admire the fruits of a new generation's youthful enterprise, to offer advice when he was asked it, and to be silent as they made their mistakes, had their squabbles, and found ways of making up again.

He was content, too, to know that just as he had always been welcome in the Badger's new home, till that great animal passed on, so he was welcome still at Toad's Palace, though that animal was less and less seen now, since he had rediscovered the pleasures of European travel. Needless to say, from what the Mole heard when Master Toad came visiting to check on the estate, his pater was still capable of causing as much mayhem and amusement in those sunny resorts as he always had along the River Bank.

The Mole's greatest contentment of all, however, came from having been taken into the happy home that his Nephew had created with another – one of those of the female kind of whom the Mole and his River Bank friends had always been so wary.

He was glad that Nephew took so bold a plunge, and gladder still that Nephew should so often sing his praises, and make him feel, old and infirm though he was, part and parcel of his growing family.

If Nephew's wife had been unsure about letting his uncle move in with them at first, how soon she, too, grew to love the Mole when she saw how readily he took to his great-nephews and -nieces, and how readily they took to him. Many were the nights that Nephew and his wife found themselves lingering at their children's bedroom doors, or near the warmth of the fireside, to hear the Mole tell once more some oft-told tale of the Water Rat, or of Mr Badger, or of Mr Toad of Toad Hall.

The Mole found a happiness and contentment there he never thought he could find, or even knew existed. A home not quite like his own Mole End, yet just as comfortable, and just as welcoming; and a family as

lively, as loving, as full of fun as any he could have
wished to have had himself.

A frequent visitor was their neighbour Grandson,
whom folk in those parts had begun now to call Badger,
for he had many of the virtues of his grandfather, not
least of which was an interest in study and learning, and
a calm wisdom beyond his years.

There was one other who was part of their new life, as
he had been of their old: Portly. The newer generation,
such as Nephew's children, were encouraged to call
Portly "Mr Otter", or "Otter" when they got to know
him better. The older and more enquiring amongst
them could not for one moment imagine where Portly
had gained his nickname, for by then he was already
lean and lithe as adult otters are and, like his father, he
was bigger and stronger than most.

With respect to the fate of the Otter, Portly's father,
nothing was heard till one June, when two years after the
Badger's death, an itinerant pedlar from Lathbury
brought news that Otter of the River Bank was no
more. Where or how he had passed on was not known,
but certainly a traveller from the southern coast *had*
reported that an otter who answered to Mr Otter's
description had lived there for a time, and he had often
been seen in the creeks and inlets fishing in a blue-and-
white inland craft.

"Ratty's boat!" whispered the Mole when he heard
this news, and if he wept quiet tears it was as much for
happy memory as for sad loss, and gladness to know that
his friend's beloved boat had seen out its last years in the
care of one such as the Otter.

It gave him special comfort, for Ratty still held as dear a place in the Mole's heart as he ever had, and always would. Long, long had that traveller's silence been, and Mole had very nearly given up all hope of hearing from him again – not because he doubted Ratty's affection for him, not one bit, but because it seemed likely that somewhere out on the High Seas, or maybe in a far distant port, the Rat had reached the end of his travels, and his life.

The Mole was realistic in this regard, and hoped that whatever had finally happened to his old friend was short, swift and, well – adventurous and exciting – and that it happened only after he had seen those many places he had marked off on the atlas that the Mole kept by his bed, for nightly perusal and dreaming.

So it was with considerable surprise and relief that two years after the Rat's departure, a missive found its way to Nephew's home in an envelope much stamped and over-stamped, and re-addressed from Mole End, with the strange note: *"Addressee believed deceased, try his nephew, care of Lathbury Forest."*

The letter was from the Rat and had been written only a few months after he had left the River Bank, and it was short and to the point:

Dear Mole,
Have made landfall in Cyprus having lost Sea Rat to the pirates of Istanbul. Getting up a command to rescue him. Am well and hope you are too. Your friend Ratty. PS. will get my journal copied and sent to you for safekeeping.
Ratty

It was three more years before the Rat was heard of again, and as for the journal, that did not arrive. Then, quite suddenly, two more short missives turned up, one marked *"Delayed by Rough Seas"*. The first came from Al Basrah in the Persian Gulf to say that the Rat had joined the Caliph's Court as Tutor in Nautical Matters to his eighteen male heirs; and the second, dated nearly two years on, brought the news that he had *"escaped the Caliph's dungeons and lately arrived in Penang to claim my reward for rescuing the Australian High Commissioner from brigands."*

It pleased the Mole to see that the Rat's handwriting was as firm as it had ever been, and to know that his friend had found at last that excitement and adventure he had always dreamed of.

But after that there had been no more letters, none at all, and in the secret silence of his heart the Mole rather feared that there never would be. But he was happy to have as a final memory of his friend and erstwhile companion in adventure the image of him rescuing an important personage "from brigands".

It cannot fairly be said the Mole ever went into decline. He moved about a bit more stiffly, yet move about he did. He saw more dimly, yet still well enough to enjoy a view, and the sight of his growing grandchildren's faces. He heard less well, but not so badly that he could not be woken by the morning chorus, or hear the nightjar's song as he sat in the porch of an evening with Nephew, with a rug over his knees and sipping a warming drink.

"Yet he seems suddenly so sad and silent, and will

hardly speak to me anymore, which is most unlike him," Nephew told his wife one September day. "It'll be his birthday at the end of the month and I would like to find out what's wrong before then and put it right. Why don't you talk to him?"

Nephew's wife did not have to wait long for an opportune moment. The very next morning, soon after Nephew had gone off for the day, the postman delivered a letter for the Mole, and it was plain enough who it was from, since the stamps, this time, were Egyptian, and the letter, as before, was re-addressed from Mole End.

The Mole opened the letter with strange foreboding, for his name and original address were not in the Rat's familiar hand. But the contents were, though it took some moments for the Mole to see that the thin and straggling writing therein was Ratty's, but of a Ratty all too plainly ill and ailing.

Dear Mole,

I am ill with the Gruesome in Cairo just as Sea Rat once was and unlikely to see the light of tomorrow. Have missed you and the River Bank these months past and have wanted to come home. If I ever recover I will do so, but it seems unlikely. Please say goodbye to the old place for me and sit on the bank once more and commune with her I loved so much – the River.

Yours always

Ratty

The Mole wept then, wept as he never had before, shedding all those tears he had held back since Ratty had left the River Bank.

He sniffled and wept, and wept and sniffled some more, and talked of old times, and had a little to eat and some fresh-brewed tea.

Finally he said, "I'm just a silly old mole, aren't I? For times change and we must all pass on in the end."

"You're not silly at all!" replied Nephew's wife firmly. "That's not a word any of us would *ever* apply to you!"

"Help me on with my coat, my dear," said the Mole, "for I have a fancy to take a turn along the River."

"Shall I come with you?"

"I would be glad if you would," said he, suddenly feeling old and frail.

The grateful Mole led her outside and down to the River, which flowed faster here than it had on the River Bank, whose willows were replaced here with larger trees, their leaves just beginning to turn to autumn colour.

The Mole stood watching the water's flow for a long time, the Rat's fateful letter in one hand, as he leant on a stick with the other.

"Ratty used to be able to commune with the River," he said, "and said very often that she will tell you what you need to hear, if only – if –"

"What is it, Mole?" said she, coming closer, for his voice was fainter now.

"There have been times when I myself have heard the River's song," he said, almost in a whisper, "and I must have told you that it was she who told me to encourage Ratty to go off on his travels, and I did, I did. Then, when he left in his boat with the Sea Rat I heard her song of farewell – except that – except –"

The letter fluttered suddenly from his hand and he dropped the stick and moved closer to the edge.

"Except what, Mole, *what?*"

"Except that she did not sing of farewell at all, but of a safe return, that one day when his travels were all done Ratty would come back home, and – and I can hear her now – I am sure. Where is that letter? Let me see it once more!"

She found it on the ground and gave it back to him, and restored his stick as well.

He peered at it and said, "There! It was written not six months since, and though he was ill I am sure he might have recovered, just as the Sea Rat did. Yes – I am sure – I think."

He sat down then upon the bank, just as he so often had by Ratty's house, and Nephew's wife might have sat by him then had not Nephew himself come by.

"Let him be," he said, putting a restraining hand upon his wife's arm, "for he is communing with the River, just as Ratty so often did. Let him be still and hear her song once more."

So the Mole sat, listening as best he could, waving his hands and arms about as the Rat always had, all the better to win out of the River her sweet and secret song of guidance and truth for those she loved.

Till at last he sat still, his head low, nodding sometimes, his hands falling to his sides. Then he slowly stood up and turned to them, his eyes clear, his expression certain, and purposeful.

"It's Ratty," he said at last, "he's safe now, but he's not well, not well at all. He's coming home at last, and I must be there to greet him. I must be there."

No more words were needed to convince Nephew of the seriousness with which his uncle spoke. Mole had been such a stalwart friend to others in the past, never judging them, always patient with them; now he would need a little help himself, for he could not return to the River Bank on his own, without support.

"Leave it to me, Uncle, I shall arrange it at once and we shall have you there for your birthday."

"My birthday!" exclaimed the Mole. "He never once forgot it. If he is coming back, as I am sure he is, then he will want to be back for that. O yes, he'll do his best to be back for that!"

* * *

Nephew summoned Portly, Grandson and Master Toad to a conference at once, where all agreed that they would accompany the Mole back to his old home for a day or two and let it be his birthday treat, for no one deserved one more.

It added very greatly to the pleasures of his birthday week that Mr Toad himself, suffering just lately from a touch of gout arising from a heavy social schedule in Biarritz, had come home for a cure and some quiet living. Though he was now confined to a Bath chair, it did not stop him visiting his old friend the Mole, and, when he heard what the younger folk planned for him, he made sure that he was there in person to wave him farewell.

"Mole, old chap," cried Toad on the morning of their departure, "if I could come back with you to the River Bank I would, but as I can't I'll toast your health every day this week!"

"But, Toad," responded the Mole, "haven't the doctors suggested that your gout might be connected in some way to excesses of one kind and another, including – ?"

"Pooh!" said Toad dismissively. "Doctors are unspeakable fellows who line their own pockets by giving advice that serves only to make their clients' lives miserable. My gout has nothing to do with my consumption of champagne and port, and everything to do with the strains and stresses of deteriorating service in the hotels upon the Continent. Therefore, toast you I shall – and as much as I like!"

"Well, that's very kind of you, but –" essayed the Mole, seeking another form of words that might put some sense into the mind of the incorrigible Toad.

"Have a good time, Mole," said Toad, rising from his Bath chair and embracing him, which he had never in his life done before. "For without you and Mole End I do not think the River Bank would have been the same or so much fun –"

"Why, Toad!" cried the Mole, surprised and moved by this unexpected speech. "I do believe –"

"Nonsense!" said Toad, collapsing back into his invalid conveyance and wiping away the tears that the Mole had seen. "Now, be off with you, and watch over him, you fellows, for he is a friend of Mr Toad's!"

Then it was that the Mole was bundled into Master Toad's latest car and found himself waving goodbye to

Nephew's wife and children, and a blubbering Toad as well. They picked up Portly and the Badger on the way and before Mole knew it, or could protest further, he was bowling along the road, the wind in his hair, and Master Toad was commanding the others to see to their guest's every need.

"Give him champagne!" said Master Toad, just as Toad would have done.

"But I oughtn't – well, just a sip," said Mole, just as he always had.

"Give him a Havana!"

"But I have never – well, just a puff, if you insist."

"Give him the map – because we're lost!"

"All in all," declared the Mole when they arrived at the Hat and Boot for the night and he found himself treated like a celebrity, and given the finest, most rumbustious birthday supper he could ever recall, "all in all, Master Toad – or Toad as everyone else now seems to call you – you are not as bad a driver as I had feared when we set off and you lost the way."

"Not as bad as Mr Toad, eh?" laughed Master Toad.

"Never as bad as that!" declared the happy and excited Mole.

Next day, they dawdled on the way, taking an early lunch at that old farmhouse where so long before the Mole and the Water Rat had stayed, and Mr Toad and Master Toad had duped the farmer's wife and his daughter into giving them room and board for a few days before the farmer returned and threw them both in the River. Now that daughter was a plump matron, with children of her own, and her parents long since passed away.

But what a welcome she gave them, and how honoured she felt to have such an eminent and venerable guest at her table as Mr Mole himself!

"Not long now, Mole," cried Master Toad as they set off once more, "not more than half an hour."

"We are certainly travelling very fast," said the Mole.

"Can't beat a vehicle like this," said Master Toad, "nothing's better, nothing – is – more – fun –"

The vehicle shuddered, it slewed, something exploded somewhere deep inside, and finally it gasped and stopped.

"Humph!" said Master Toad. "Wait till I see that salesman!"

So it was that they made the last part of the journey on foot, arriving by way of the bank that ran opposite what had once been Toad Hall, and which they saw had been turned into the Wild Wood Preparatory School for Children of the Gentry, with what had been Toad's fine lawns turned now into a sports field, and every sign that the old boat-house now housed the School Rowing Club.

The Iron Bridge soon came into view, and here the company split in two, for though the Mole's main purpose was to see if there were any signs of life at the Rat's House, he was anxious first to go to Mole End and see what had become of it.

"Let's meet back here at the Iron Bridge at ten o'clock tomorrow morning," said Master Toad. "By then my motor-car may be repaired."

So Master Toad, Portly and Grandson headed off to the Village to find their own accommodation, while the

Mole and Nephew set off to find out what they might about the fate of Mole End.

The old path had gone, fenced off now by new palings, and not much further down the road they saw an intriguing new notice.

"Good heavens!" exclaimed the Mole on reading it, for its words were clear and unequivocal:

MOLE END

*The property of the National Trust for Historical Buildings
and Natural Scenery: This way.
(Parties of over twenty only by prior arrangement.
Charabancs not to block the road.)*

They opened the gate and set off along a newly surfaced path fenced on either side by iron railings.

"Well, it seems that Mole End is still there," said the Mole with barely concealed excitement. "Though I cannot say that I like this new path much. Might we not go the old way?"

They found a spot where the railings were loose, and with a little push and shove were through it and walking along that path they had so often walked together after a day or evening with their friends, which ran along the River for a little way before turning amongst the hedgerows towards Mole End.

The Mole chose to linger awhile near the River, and for the first time in the course of the expedition, Nephew noticed that he seemed a little tired, and that the excitement that had taken so many years from his face had worn thin. He sat a little hunched, staring into

271

the placid water, listening to sounds so long familiar.

Nephew feared that worse might follow before long, for he had not had the heart to say that it seemed unlikely to him that Ratty really would be back, and the most the Mole could gain from the trip was fulfilment of his desire to say a final goodbye to the River Bank.

The Mole's mood was not helped by the sight of the clipped municipal grass on the other bank, and beyond, where the Wild Wood had been, the thin young ornamental trees and grass of suburban parkland, a children's playground and the first of those houses compulsorily developed in partnership by the Town Authority and the High Judge's consortium.

But on *his* side all was still much as it had been, and the Mole sat enjoying it, wistful and thoughtful, suddenly old.

"Come on, Nephew, help me up from here, for I have seen what I came to see of this part and rather fear to venture on. Yet perhaps we shall not be disappointed."

They turned the last corner back to the new-made path and there they saw another notice, on a neat and freshly painted little booth: *1/- adults, 6d juveniles (under age 10) In absence of Curator or his assistant place ticket money in slot and take one sheet per person.*

"Stranger and stranger," said Nephew, "but I really don't think we need to —"

"If you have the change, Nephew, then please do pay the entrance fee, for someone is certainly maintaining the old place and that costs money."

There was a twinkle in the Mole's eye, for he rather enjoyed the notion that Mole End had become a destination for charabanc parties and day trippers.

Nephew had taken up one of the leaflets and now began to read aloud from it:

> *"Mole End was for many years the permanent residence of Mr Mole, the close friend and confidant of the internationally renowned sportsman and financier, Mr Toad, who lived nearby at Toad Hall. These two gentlemen, along with Mr Badger of the Wild Wood, Mr Rat of the River Bank and their associate Mr Otter, formed the core of that group of individuals now generally known as the River-Bankers.*
>
> *"Visitors to Mole End are thus afforded a unique opportunity to gain an insight into the personal lives of a community long gone, and a way of life from a different (and some might say better) age . . . "*

"It rather seems," observed the Mole wryly, "that the gentleman who wrote those words thinks that Mr Mole is dead."

"O, he *is* dead, sir, dead and buried long ago!"

This sudden and surprising interruption came from a figure wearing a navy blue hat with a hard shiny visor, whose head had appeared out of the Mole's former bedroom window.

"I am the Curator, Mr Adams, and I welcome you."

His head disappeared, the window closed and moments later out he popped into the open, where they saw that his uniform extended to a blue serge jacket and trousers, and very shiny boots. He had a cheerful smile, and held a duster in his hand.

"It's always good to see moles coming to visit," he said, "for it goes to show what I've always said: one day his own kind will appreciate what a fine and sterling animal Mr Mole was, and quite equal in his way to Mr Toad himself."

"Well, I wouldn't quite go so far as that!" exclaimed the Mole, much flattered by the Curator's remark.

"That's because you don't know all of Mr Mole's life history, sir, if I might be so bold. You've probably just heard of him as being a friend of Mr Rat, or 'Ratty' as we believe Mr Mole called him, and one of those who appeared from time to time in the larger story of Mr Toad's illustrious life."

"Well, I –" began the Mole, but the Curator was not to be stopped.

"But if you'll come this way, sir, I'll show you round while I tell you something of Mr Mole's life and heroic death."

"Heroic death!" exclaimed Nephew, tempted to reveal who the Mole was but stopped from doing so by a frown from the Mole, who proposed to enjoy listening to the history of his life and death.

"Now you will observe before we enter the house itself, this little garden, and that bench there, which is where Mr Mole was wont to sit taking tea with Mr Rat. We have no documentary evidence that this happened, only the memories of the grandparents of some of the local inhabitants."

The Mole remembered those rabbits to whom he and nephew had given the key of Mole End when they left so hurriedly.

"You have kept it very well," said the Mole, looking about his old garden and glad to observe that the statues of Queen Victoria and Garibaldi in which he had always taken so much pride were still in place, and that the urn full of flowers was very much as he had left it.

"We pride ourselves on preserving things as they were," said the Curator. "I believe that were Mr Mole alive today he would not want things changed and modernized. Mind you, some improvements had to take place – like that path. In the old days that did not exist but in high season we have so many visitors that we felt it best to keep them to one path.

"But Mr Mole liked his home comforts, and he liked tradition. He was a proper gentleman and treated his guests properly whoever they might be. Well, now he has gone we must try to do the same for him, and treat his home just as he would have liked us to. Perhaps you would care to follow me inside?"

The Curator went on ahead while the Mole lingered for a moment, as much to brush the ready tears that had come from the words just spoken so feelingly, as to look again at the garden and that bench where he and Ratty had spent so many happy hours.

Once inside, the Curator took them to the kitchen, the parlour and the bedrooms, all of which were in perfect order, just as the Mole had left them so many years before. Here and there a few items seemed to have been added which were not originally there: some coal and logs by the fire grate, for example, and by the Mole's old bed some dried flowers.

"My son found those by the River Bank and we felt sure that Mr Mole would have approved."

"O, he would, I'm sure he would," said the Mole happily, turning about, poking here and there, and drawing Nephew's attention to so many things that brought memories flooding back.

"Tell me about Mr Mole's death, if you please," said the Mole quietly.

"You will have heard of the historic battle of Lathbury Chase, perhaps – that same battle in which the great Mr Toad himself was at the forefront?"

"Er, indeed –" began the Mole, not sure what to say.

"I have good reason to believe that Mr Mole was one of the anonymous slain upon that bloody fell, and was buried there in a mass grave, with friend and foe alike, the site now quite forgotten."

"That is a very great pity," observed the Mole.

"It is, sir, for as Curator of Mole End, there are a good many questions I would like to have asked him."

"Such as?" said the obliging Mole.

"Well, for one thing, sir, I could never quite fathom why he had a statue of Garibaldi in his garden."

"I believe that radical Italian was a hero of Mr Mole's radical youth," said the Mole.

"I see, hmm, an interesting theory," observed the Curator thoughtfully.

"What else would you like to know?" said the Mole, taking off his coat.

"Ah, well now, what I would *very* much like to know, though I fear I never will, for the secret died with him, is his recipe for *this*!"

The Curator went to the Mole's old dresser, and drew out a bottle, dusty with age, which he placed on the table before the Mole.

The Mole picked up the bottle and examined it.

"Be careful, sir, that is the very last known bottle of Mr Mole's famous Sloe and Blackberry!"

"And one of the very finest vintages!" said the Mole.

"You are an expert on such things, sir?"

"I am an expert on *this*," said the Mole with truth. "Indeed, some might say that no one has ever made it better than I, eh Nephew?"

"Did you say *Nephew,* sir?" said the Curator, light beginning to dawn.

"Have you a paper and pencil?" asked the generous Mole. "Then I'll give you the recipe!"

As Mole sat at his own kitchen table, slowly and carefully writing down the precious recipe, the Curator stared from one to the other, and back again, not daring to interrupt, nor to believe what he was beginning to think.

"There," said the Mole at last, "and don't believe it when people say you must have almonds in it, for it's just not true. But the main thing is to pick your sloes from the blackthorn bushes that grow on the left side of the path going down to the River, and to do so as soon after the first heavy frost of autumn as you can, for then the sloes are ready to release their colour and their goodness, and there is no need to prick them one by one, which you will know to be a tiresome task if you have ever tried to do it. Now, was there anything else?"

The Curator decided that he would not risk asking the Mole outright if he was who he thought, as if it might break the spell in some way, but he begged leave to ask in his children that they might meet him, and listen to him, and then to ask one last question.

"And what is that?"

"I have never been able to work out how it came to pass that Mr Mole first met Mr Water Rat. Would it have been here, perhaps, when that practical gentleman was in search of someone to help with his boat, or down there on the River Bank, where Mr Mole might have been strolling along one day?"

The Mole stared at him a long time in silence.

"Nephew," said the Mole at last, "I fancy we shall need some tea by and by, and perhaps a fire lit in the grate, for it is autumn now, and the nights are getting cold."

Nephew rose to see what he could find in the way of tea and biscuits. Meanwhile the Mole got up from the table and sat down in his old armchair, and asked that the Curator sit in the other, and said, "Now, let me try to tell you how Mr Mole first met Ratty.

"You see, he had been working hard all morning, spring-cleaning his little home. First with brooms, then with dusters; then on ladders. O, but spring was moving in the air above and in the earth below, penetrating even his dark and lowly little house with its spirit of divine discontent and longing —"

So the Mole began the story of his first meeting with the Water Rat, and if in the course of its telling Nephew, having lit the fire and made them tea, later quietly opened the bottle that the Curator had been guarding for so many years, and which had seemed irreplaceable, surely none of them could think that such an elixir was for keeping in a museum, but rather that it was much better drunk in good company.

In any case, more could always be made, and one day,

however long it might take, wherever it might be, there would be another vintage year to rival that which the Mole remembered so well, and which he recounted now with such love – which was the year he met the Water Rat, who introduced him to the River, and all the wonders that lay Beyond.

EPILOGUE
Beyond

Evening came, and the Mole declared himself to be somewhat tired.

"It won't take more than a moment to get Mr Mole's bed made up, nor his Nephew's either," said the Curator, who still pretended not to know who they were. "It's against the rules, no doubt, but who is there here to find out but ourselves? In any case, sir, if I might say so, Mr Mole would never have turned you out into an autumn night."

"But we must be up before the dawn," said the Mole, "for we have a last task to perform down by the River on behalf of a friend, to say goodbye and give thanks for what we once had."

"You'll need to be gone early in any case, sir, for tomorrow's Saturday and we have a charabanc coming from the Town at half past nine. We'll have breakfast ready and waiting at sunrise."

How well Mole and Nephew slept that night; how good to hear the sounds they had heard so often before: the tawny owl calling, the bark of the fox, and far off, low and whispering, the sounds of autumn coming, and the wind in the willows along the River Bank.

The Curator was as good as his word, and though Nephew had a hearty breakfast, the Mole had little more than a cup of tea and a piece of toast.

"It's a misty morning, sir, and chilly with it, but a bit of walking will warm you up."

"Yes," said the Mole quietly, wondering if he had quite the strength to walk so far.

"What is it, Uncle?"

The Mole put on his old coat and scarf, and opened his front door. It was cold, quite; it was misty, very.

"Uncle, are you all right?"

"Can you not hear her voice, Nephew; can you not hear her song?"

He barely said goodbye to the Curator before he was off into the strange dawn light, leaving Nephew to say his "thankyou's" for him.

"He's not normally like this, you know, but he seems a trifle over-wrought this morning, and still a little tired."

"It has been a pleasure, sir, to meet you and that gentleman, who was so kind to tell me what he knew of Mr Mole."

Then the Curator winked, and chuckled, for he knew quite well who his special guest had been. Then, laughing, Nephew followed his uncle down the familiar path towards the River.

"Uncle, Uncle!" he called, for the mist was strange and swirling, and he was suddenly not sure quite how far down the path the Mole had gone. *"Uncle, wait for me!"*

Down the path he went, almost running, yet not quite catching up with the familiar form of the Mole, whose head he saw, and then his scarf, and the shape of his coat – and a singing, a voice, a song of calling, a song of sweet belonging and of return.

"I'm coming, Uncle," cried Nephew. "I'm not far behind. The sun will soon be out and we'll be able to see more clearly, and then, then – "

Nephew paused and came to a stop, for already he had reached the River and what he saw a little way below, still vague and misty was rather more than the Mole.

It seemed to be a rowing boat, a boat that might well have been moored and waiting, waiting for minutes or hours, days or years – but even now was casting off as it so often had of yore, as the River's song grew louder, and the sun so bright in the mist that it was hard to see – and hard for Nephew to quite comprehend what he was seeing.

For there in the blue-and-white boat he knew so well was the Mole, in the seat in which he had sat so many times before, and sitting opposite him, oars confidently in his hands once more, was one who seemed to be the Water Rat.

"Ratty?" whispered Nephew in awe as the light came all about them, and the River's song grew loud. "Uncle?"

For a moment the Rat turned to stare at him, and the Mole too, and on their faces there was a look of sweet companionship and contentment, and in their silence the calling of farewell.

Then, even as the mist cleared by the bank, the boat drifted out into the River and turned towards the Island with the River's eternal flow.

"Uncle?" whispered Nephew once more, and he saw on the path, and down by the water, the hoof-marks of some great animal, and knew that He was near.

"Farewell!" sang the River, her voice joining at last with Ratty and Mole's. "Farewell!"

The song rose all about Nephew as he watched and saw the boat drift onward, and the mist broke up ever more, yet never quite enough for him to see all clearly.

He stood in silence as the boat reached the Island, and the song changed from farewell to welcome. Though he could not be sure, Nephew felt certain he saw Badger waiting there, and Otter too, and Ratty helping Mole from the boat; yes, and there was Toad, younger than Nephew had ever known him, calling to them to hurry up and hurry along, for he had an idea for them, and it started just over there on the other side of the Island, just over there, just Beyond.

So Toad had now made the final journey too . . .

Nephew sat down and watched the mist slowly clear down towards the Island and the Weir. He stared at the water, and thought of many things.

He peered across the River to where once the Wild Wood had risen up. But as yet that was still in mist, and there was nothing to be seen. Yet the sun was all about him, and the autumn wind so mild, and the leaves of willows on the River, floating, falling, drifting –

"Nephew? Is that really you?"

He awoke with a start, and thought himself still lost in that world of Beyond, for there in the middle of the River was a water rat, standing up in a skiff quite different from Ratty's boat, yet one he knew, for he remembered Young Rat making it, many years before.

Nephew stood up.

"Hullo, Young Rat," he said without surprise, as if he had expected him to be there. "So you came back home?"

"Came back a few days ago, Ratty and I, and have been waiting ever since, for it's Mr Mole's birthday today and Ratty was sure Mr Mole would return, for the River told him so. She's been singing a song of long-ing all the way up from the coast, and Ratty's been so impatient. But now – now – "

Young Rat looked down the River the way Mole and Ratty had gone.

"Did you see them?" he whispered, idling the oar in the River to bring himself nearer to where Nephew sat.

"Yes," said Nephew, "O yes, I did."

Young Rat brought the boat to the bank and lightly jumped off. Little wonder that Nephew had mistaken him for Ratty a moment before: he was wearing one of Ratty's old tweed suits.

"Found it in his old home," said Young Rat, as he once had been, but Rat as he now surely was.

"Did you?" said Nephew.

They sat in silence for a time, wondering. Talk could come later but for now the River's song was still in their ears, and the cloven hoof had not long passed by.

"Rat, old fellow," said Nephew, feeling as easy with his old friend as if they had never parted, "would you mind just taking me down to the Island, just for a little —"

But something impelled the Rat to shake his head slowly, for Mole and Ratty could not be followed to the place where they had gone.

They heard then the River's song all about them, and though afterwards they could not quite remember it, knew more then of fulfilment, and the true meaning of Beyond; and while Nephew listened in wonder, and watched the shifting light in strange delight, the Rat sculled to the Island and there, without once setting foot upon that hallowed place, or even glancing in amongst the vegetation there, grasped the painter of Ratty's boat, and brought it back to Nephew, and to mortality, again.

Later, leaving that part of the bank, with their farewells to the past and to Mole, Ratty and all the old River-Bankers quite done, the two friends crossed over to Ratty's house, his old boat in tow. They clambered up onto the jetty and sat with their feet dangling, just as Ratty and Mole often had. Of the past there was nothing left to say, and it was to the future that their thoughts now bent.

"Did you find a new home, Nephew, and is there room there for a wanderer like me?"

"We did," said Nephew with a smile, "and there is! But hold fast a moment, what's the time?"

The Rat pulled from his pocket a silver watch that had once been Ratty's and said, "Almost ten o'clock."

"Then we must get to the Iron Bridge without delay for Toad – that's Master Toad as was, and Badger – that's –"

"I know who that must be," said the Rat with a grin. "Tell me the rest when you're aboard or we'll never get there in time."

"But Ratty's house?"

"It's all locked up, and there's a note for the rabbits to look after it, and the key as well. All I need is already stowed aboard my skiff."

How expertly the Rat managed the boat; how easily he began to row; and how comfortable Nephew's seat felt, as the River glided by, and they left their past behind.

"There they are!" cried Nephew, spying Master Toad, Badger and Portly. "But no motor-car, I'm afraid. They can't have repaired it."

Such explanations as could be swiftly made, were made. Such apologies as could be made, Toad made, for his vehicle had had to be sent back to the Town and they would have to walk.

"Nonsense, we'll go by boat," said the practical Rat. "Portly, or should I say Otter, you and Toad take the skiff, for you'll know how to handle her, and take Badger with you, for he'll be able to keep Toad under control. I'll take this boat with Neph – with *Mole*."

"All the way home by boat?" cried Toad doubtfully.

"Better than hiking," said Otter with a grin.

"Humph," said Toad ruefully.

But then, as the two craft cast off, and the Rat led them towards the darkness beneath the Iron Bridge, a peaceful look came to Toad's eyes and he let his fingers trail in the water.

"I've always liked boats," said he, "but it's a long time since I had one. I think I'll buy a few."

"One's enough," said the Badger gruffly, "and prefer-ably without an engine, for they don't break down."

"I don't suppose they do," said Toad dreamily. Then, a moment later, he added, "You know, you're right. Can't beat boats."

"Won't ever beat boats," said the Rat.

"Hear, hear!" said the Mole.

Then they were gone, Mole and Toad, Badger and Rat, and Otter too, gone under the Iron Bridge and away upstream towards Lathbury Forest, heading home, there to find out all the wonders of what might await them in the future, and Beyond.

THE END

Acknowledgements

A book such as this, even more a series such as *Tales of the Willows*, cannot be brought to successful publication without the creative and practical help of a great many people. Six in particular should be mentioned by name.

First, my warm gratitude to Eddie Bell, Executive Chairman and Publisher of HarperCollins, who in a two-minute telephone conversation in 1993 saw at once the essence of the idea and immediately gave it approval and support, as he has ever since. That is real publishing.

My special thanks to Patrick Benson, whose accompanying illustrations have rightly earned him such international acclaim. Thanks also to Ian Craig, who as art director of the project has been responsible for its overall look, which captures so well the spirit of the famous 1932 edition of Kenneth Grahame's *The Wind in the Willows* illustrated by Ernest Shepard, and takes it forward so brilliantly to something new.

I have been exceptionally lucky in the two editors – Malcolm Edwards and Tim Waller – who have been closely involved in the series since its inception, and have guided my words and ideas into print with such common sense and good humour.

Finally, as so often on these occasions – and so happily – to Deborah Crawshaw, my partner, who recently became my wife. She has shared my laughter and occasional tears with Mole, Ratty, Badger and Toad.

I have received many hundreds of comments about these books from readers and others, but by far the most charming came from my young son Joshua, who, listening to Richard Briers' tape of the first volume in the series, *The Willows in Winter*, summoned me to his side and said, "Daddy, why don't you try to write something like this?"

We fathers, like us storytellers, can only try.

William Horwood
Oxford
July 1996

Join Mole, *Toad*, *Ratty*, and *Badger* for more unforgettable adventures...

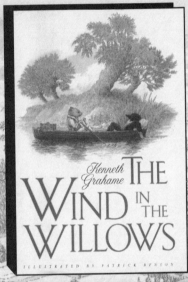

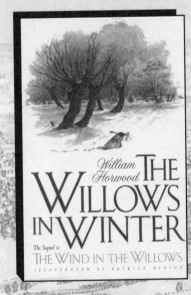

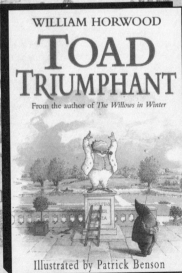

All available in hardcover
and paperback